BREAKFAST AT THE BUTTERSCOTCH BAKERY

Following a skiing accident, Connie is laid up in Switzerland with a badly broken leg. Stepping into the breach, her sister has promised to run her business, the Butterscotch Bakery, during her convalescence. After all, Kaley's a capable computer programmer, and it's not exactly rocket science to rustle up a few cupcakes and coffees . . . is it? But baking's not as simple as it looks – and when Kaley comes unstuck, handsome customer Jacca is there to lend a hand . . .

ANGELA BRITNELL

BREAKFAST AT THE BUTTERSCOTCH BAKERY

Complete and Unabridged

LINFORD
Leicester

First published in Great Britain in 2020

First Linford Edition
published 2021

*A catalogue record for this book is available
from the British Library.*

ISBN 978–1–4448–4771–0

Published by
Ulverscroft Limited
Anstey, Leicestershire

Printed and bound in Great Britain by
TJ Books Ltd., Padstow, Cornwall

This book is printed on acid-free paper

Big Challenge Ahead

Seriously? Who needs to eat breakfast at six in the morning?

Kaley hit the snooze button for the third time, smashed a warm comfy pillow around her head and burrowed down. Two seconds later her mother's chiding voice crept in there, too.

'Don't be late opening up. I'll be there as soon as I can but it all depends how your father's doing.'

Instead of flying back to San Francisco to resume work after the Christmas holidays, she would do her best to keep the Butterscotch Bakery solvent until Connie got back on her feet. Literally. Her unco-ordinated younger sister had decided to impress her waste-of-space boyfriend out skiing and the result was a badly broken leg that would take the best part of two months to heal.

Connie was stuck in Switzerland for at least a fortnight until the doctors authorised her to fly back to Nashville.

Kaley flung back the covers and rushed to the bathroom for the quickest shower on record. She pulled on old jeans, a baggy turquoise jumper and sensible sneakers before yanking her hair back in a hygienic ponytail.

In the last few seconds of free time she added a sweep of mascara and dark red lipstick, the least make-up she'd faced the rest of the world in since she was twelve years old.

At least her new commute was straight forward. Step One — leave Connie's apartment. Step Two — run downstairs to the bakery.

Half an hour later she abandoned doing battle with the oven. For someone who programmed computers for a living it shouldn't be complicated but she couldn't even locate the on/off switch.

She reluctantly unlocked the shop door although there was nothing ready to serve apart from cold drinks and pre-packaged cookies.

'Um, excuse me but are you open? The sign says you are but . . . '

'There's no smell of freshly baked muffins or fragrant coffee brewing?' She glared at the man hovering outside the door. 'Aren't you clever? Come in or we'll freeze.'

'Very doubtful.' The red woolly hat he tugged off revealed a mass of matching curly hair to go with his appealing smile and lean freckled face. 'It's nearly five degrees out there.'

'Five degrees? You're crazy. There's no snow and ice on the ground.'

'I suspect we're talking at cross purposes. You're speaking in Fahrenheit and I'm fluent in Celsius.' His bright blue eyes sparkled.

'The warnings about transatlantic travel never cover these kinds of minefields. I'm Jacca Hawken by the way. Temporary Nashville resident but . . .' He leaned in closer. 'In my heart I'm a Cornish pirate. If you're running low on French brandy and silk stockings I'm your man.'

If she wasn't an obsessive fan of the Poldark books and television series Kaley would consider him totally deranged.

'Can pirates knock disobedient ovens into shape, Mr Hawken?'

'They can do anything, Ms . . . we didn't finish the whole introduction thing.'

'Kaley Robertson.'

'Good heavens, girl, haven't you got things underway yet?' A short, bleached blonde whirlwind breezed in. 'Hasn't my daughter served you yet?' Lorna homed in on Jacca.

Kaley caught his curious glance. The lack of physical resemblance between them couldn't be more obvious. She owed her tall curvy figure and caramel skin to her Jamaican birth mother and the blonde hair to her Norwegian father. Describing her background as complicated didn't come close.

'Apparently there's a problem with the oven,' Jacca explained.

'Sit down, hon, and I'll sort things out. Coffee?'

'Thank you.' He draped his long black wool coat over the back of the nearest chair and sat down. Kaley noticed his bright red plastic clogs, the same style her sister wore for working in the kitchen. They were popular these days and suited his quirky appearance.

'Stop drooling over the customers. We've got work to do.' Lorna steered her towards the kitchen.

'If we're being grammatically correct it should be customer. Singular. There's only one of him.' Thank goodness. 'And I wasn't drooling, simply being polite.'

Her mother raised her eyebrows. Lorna Robertson hadn't given birth to Kaley but knew her adopted daughter inside and out.

'Right.' Her soft drawl spoke volumes. She casually turned a series of knobs on the massive stainless steel oven. 'I guess a PhD in computer science doesn't cover such mundane tasks.'

She gave a satisfied nod as it rumbled into life and performed a similar miracle on the gleaming stainless steel coffee machine.

'Find out what your red-headed cutie wants to eat and suggest a combination of eggs and bread because it'll be close to an hour before we have anything baked. Don't stand there looking at me that way, girl, shoo.'

* * *

'Hello, again, Ms Robertson or should I say Doctor? I assume you've come to get the red-headed cutie's order?' Jacca suppressed a smile when her face burned redder than his hair.

'She didn't mean any . . . she'd never have said that if she thought . . . '

'I had superhuman hearing?' His humour kicked her searing blush up another notch. 'Do scrambled eggs and whole wheat toast fit the criteria?'

'Of course. Look, I'm really sorry.'

'Hey, it's fine. I'm not in any rush but I suspect if you don't give your mother my order she'll be on your case again.'

'It's not all her fault.' The tilt of her chin forced him to keep his expression neutral in case she thought he was laughing at her.

6

Jacca never understood why men complained about women's complicated ways because to him that was their fascination. Only the other day his manager, and oldest friend in the world, discovered he'd split up with his latest girlfriend.

'When you meet one who can keep you intrigued and on your toes I'll write my best man's speech.'

Sandy's explanation was too simplistic. The root of his problem wasn't losing interest but rather the panic that sneaked in when a woman got too close for his comfort.

'I'm only running the bakery until my sister recovers from a skiing accident.' Kaley explained about Connie being stuck in Switzerland. 'Mom's got enough on her plate without worrying whether her supposedly smart daughter can rustle up a few muffins and cups of coffee. It's not rocket science ... ' A tantalising smile lit up her dark eyes. 'Although rocket science makes far more sense to me than cupcakes.'

'I might be able to help you out.'

'You?'

'Didn't you know pirates are famous for being great cooks when they're not terrorising the high seas?' Jacca caught her wary glance.

'Ah, you're one of the doubters.' He laced his voice with fake disappointment. 'I'm heading into Nashville soon but I'll be back here around eleven if that suits you?'

'Feel free if you've nothing better to do with your time.' Her dismissive tone made it clear what she thought of his offer.

'Hurry up with that poor man's order, Kaley, or he'll starve to death,' Lorna yelled.

'Don't worry, I'm not likely to fade away.' Jacca patted his stomach. She lowered her eyes and retreated to the kitchen. Time to contemplate his next move. Kaley Robertson added another level to his original plan. Unexpected, but not wholly unwelcome.

Delicious Surprise

'How's Daddy today?' Kaley watched her mother's smile fade.

'Not great.'

They had survived the breakfast crowd, although that didn't say much. The bakery was too far from the centre of Franklin to attract many casual visitors and there were barely enough regulars to keep things going.

Three years ago Connie had bought the small run-down shop with their parents' help, painted the walls a fresh mint green with bright yellow trim and filled the café with an eclectic mixture of furniture she found at yard sales. All of the shops in Dixie Street were struggling and there were no signs of the area picking up.

'Why don't you head home, Mom? I'll be fine.' They had baked enough cookies and muffins from Connie's freezer stash to get through the day but she didn't know what would happen when the supply ran out.

'Are you sure?'

'It's not a problem.'

Lorna's gaze softened.

'You're a terrible liar but a good girl.' Her mother pulled on her short denim jacket and fluffed up her hair then slicked on a fresh layer of sock-it-to-me orange lipstick. 'You'll pop in to see your daddy later?'

'Of course. Off you go.'

Kaley was finally on her own if she didn't count John Green, hunched over in the far corner of the café as if that made him invisible. He was one of Connie's habitual freeloaders and an expert at making one cup of coffee last for hours while using the free Wi-Fi.

The clock ticked towards half past 11 with no sign of her British saviour. She should've guessed. Apart from her sweet father, men usually let her down.

'Delivery for K. Robertson.' A gangly teenage boy ambled in and thrust a long white box at her. 'Sign here.'

After scrawling her name she studied the mystery package and sniffed the air when a sweet aroma seeped through the box.

She eased open the lid and found twelve beautiful cupcakes nestled in a bed of crumpled gold tissue paper. Kaley selected one and peeled off the lacy paper case. She plucked off the crispy golden shard of butterscotch stick on the top and bit it in two. One lick of the swirl of caramel icing was all it took to make her moan and she sank her teeth into the soft spicy sponge.

'Sorry I'm late but it took me a while to get the butterscotch right.' Jacca ambled in and absent-mindedly dragged off his hat and coat.

Kaley tried to wipe the tell-tale crumbs from her mouth.

'You missed a bit.' He dragged his thumb over a stray blob of icing stuck on her top lip.

'Did I?' she croaked. When she stopped staring into his bright blue eyes Jacca's words sunk in. 'Are you seriously claiming you made the cupcakes? I don't think so. You must've bought them from a fancy bakery in Nashville. Very slick to tie in the bakery name with the butter-scotch.'

'You're accusing me of being a cake smuggler?' His booming voice filled the café. 'What do you think of that, mate?'

'Me?' John Green frowned over the top of his laptop. 'I wasn't listening. I've no idea what you're talking about.'

Kaley grabbed the coffee pot and ran over to refill John's cup.

'On the house.' She swung back around and fixed her gaze on Jacca. 'Don't tell me, you're a Michelin starred pastry chef?'

His colour deepened.

'I've worked in a few kitchens and picked up stuff. That's all.

'May I take you out to dinner tonight?'

'I'm busy.'

'Genuinely busy or not interested?' Jacca persisted.

'You're relentless, aren't you? Both. Now thank you for the cupcakes but I've got work to do.'

'If you change your mind give me a

call.' He fished a business card out his wallet and dropped it on the counter then grabbed his coat and woolly hat on the way out.

She sensed it wasn't the last she'd seen of Jacca Hawken.

* * *

'Are you serious? The Red Hawk was in my bakery?' Two minutes after she sent the text message Connie was on the phone shrieking disbelief and scorn over Kaley. 'Surely even you've heard of him? Do you live under a rock in California?'

Her sister loved to exaggerate but this time her question was close to the truth. A woman like Kaley didn't crack the Silicon Valley glass ceiling by working a basic 40-hour week.

The job demanded a laser sharp focus to the detriment of any personal life and taking time off was the equivalent of career suicide. When she decided that the people she loved were more important than writing debugging code for the latest Smartphone it came with the knowledge that she might not have a job to go back to.

'He's one of the world's most awesome pastry chefs and I've heard rumours he wants to conquer America. I can't believe he's picked Nashville because everyone thought he'd target New York or LA. Is he planning to come back?'

Probably not after the way I spoke to him, Kaley thought guiltily.

'You've got his card and he asked you out,' Connie persisted. 'If you don't accept I'll never forgive you.'

'How's your leg?'

'Don't change the subject,' she chided. 'It's OK if you enjoy extreme discomfort, itching and dragging around on crutches.'

'Is Simon taking good care of you?'

'You must be joking,' Connie scoffed. 'He flew back as scheduled.'

Kaley wasn't dumb enough to comment that the man she dubbed Slimy Simon wasn't good enough for her sister in the first place.

'Don't you fancy Jacca?'

Thankfully they weren't video chatting or Kaley's burning face would confirm her sister's suspicions.

'Come on — I sneaked into a demonstration he gave at a food festival in Palm Beach last year.' Connie's throaty laugh reverberated down the phone. 'A dreamboat with a British accent who bakes like an angel. What's not to find irresistible about that?'

'OK, he is an attractive man. Are you satisfied?' No way was Kaley going to confess how Jacca Hawken had blindsided her.

'The ice queen cracks.'

'Quit it,' she snapped at her sister. 'Some of us have a ton of work to do because a certain person showed off their lack of skiing skills on a black run when they should've stayed on the bunny slopes.'

'Nasty, nasty.'

'Goodnight.' Kaley hung up before her sister could answer back. If she couldn't teach herself to bake in the next

24 hours the Butterscotch Bakery was in serious trouble.

Busted

Jacca watched downtown Nashville out of his hotel window, bustling with life despite the grey, rainy skies.

'So where were you earlier?' Sandy ambled out of his room, yawning. 'I checked on you around six o'clock to see if you wanted to order breakfast but then I guess I dozed off again.'

'Jet lag was doing me in, too, so I took our hire car and drove the twenty miles or so out to Franklin. Someone mentioned it's an interesting town and I thought I'd take a look around.'

It didn't sit easy with him to prevaricate around Sandy. He needed to check up some more on a possible business venture before broaching the subject with his old friend.

'You whiled away the whole morning there? It's one o'clock now.'

'Time slipped away.'

'I fell in line with your crazy idea to come to Music City, USA instead of one

17

of the more renowned culinary hotspots to kick start your American career but it's not going to happen without a lot of hard work.' Sandy's dark eyes narrowed. 'What aren't you telling me?'

If he admitted coming back to the hotel kitchen and talking the chef into letting him bake like a lunatic before rushing over to Franklin again, Sandy would think he'd lost the plot. He hadn't corrected Kaley's assumption that he decorated the cupcakes to match the bakery's name but in truth his inspiration came from the unusual combination of her rich coppery skin and thick honey blonde hair.

'Nothing much.' He suppressed a smile as his friend lowered his stocky frame on to one of the lightweight metal chairs.

They'd known each other since primary school in Cornwall and Sandy couldn't be a more inappropriate name for the swarthy, second-generation Sicilian but his full name, Alessandro, proved too much of a mouthful for his new classmates.

He was the middle child in a family of seven and in school his awkward bulk, thick glasses and heavy Italian accent made him a perfect target for bullies until Jacca stood up for him.

They drifted apart for a few years and crossed paths again after Sandy got his business degree and Jacca's baking career started to take off, working well together because of their shared desire to prove themselves to the world.

His own drive came from his own less than ideal childhood.

'Be realistic, son. That isn't for people like us.' His mother spouted that piece of advice the day he came home from school excited to fill in application forms for university after one teacher spotted the quick intelligence buried underneath Jacca's stroppy attitude.

He became determined to prove her wrong but although he reached the top of his profession and took care of his mother financially it made no difference to their strained relationship.

'I'll tell you what I've got lined up.'

Sandy pulled a cold soda out of the mini-bar.

'Didn't the doctor . . .'

'Do I tell you how to live your life . . . apart from when it comes to business which is what you pay me for?' He popped open the can and took a long swallow. Despite the rampant diabetes and heart disease in Sandy's family he ignored his doctor's warnings to take better care of himself. 'Listen to me.'

Jacca gave up.

* * *

A knot tightened around Kaley's heart as her father struggled to sit up.

'There's my girl. Come and sit by me.'

The worn brown leather sofa creaked when she sunk into its sagging cushions. Part of her childhood, it bore the scars of family life with two rumbustious children and their various pets. A multi-coloured afghan, hand-crocheted by her mother, covered up the worst of the damage.

'How are you today?'

'Better for seeing you.' A car crash had ended Spencer's working life ten years earlier and the after-effects were increasing with age but he rarely complained. 'Tell me what you've been up to.'

She made a joke about her English customer but skipped over the rest so he wouldn't worry about the downturn in the business.

'I'll go over and do some baking later if you sit with your daddy,' her mother offered.

'I'm not a child,' Spencer protested.

'We know that.' Kaley attempted to smooth things over. 'Thanks, Mama, but I want to have a go at trying out some new recipes. I ought to go now before it gets too late.'

'What about your dinner?'

'I'll fix something there.' If nothing else she could eat raw cake batter. Kaley gave her father a big hug and struggled to hide her shock at how insubstantial his bones felt under her fingers. 'Behave, Daddy.'

'Fat chance of doing anything else.'

'I'll see you again tomorrow.'

'If you can't manage at the bakery, Kaley, you know the ideal person to ask for help. I don't mind calling . . .'

'No, thank you.' She cut off her mother before she could mention Cash Harrison's name. Lorna would love nothing better than to help the bakery and simultaneously interfere in her daughter's private life. 'It can't be that hard to follow a recipe.'

An hour later she found out the fallacy of that statement.

Beat eggs to soft peaks and fold in. Line two 20 cm sandwich tins with parchment paper. What were sandwiches to do with cake making and did an egg beaten to soft peaks look like the Alps or Mount Everest? Was parchment paper something Egyptian?

Kaley set up her laptop and tracked down a YouTube video with step by step baking instructions. This was more like it.

★ ★ ★

Through the blinds Jacca spotted a pale yellow light glowing in the back of the shop so he strolled around the rear of the building. According to Sandy's plan this would be his last free night for several weeks because when he wasn't appearing on various radio and TV chat shows he would be busy with cooking demonstrations and meeting local chefs.

'I give up.' Kaley's irate voice drifted out through an open window and the door slammed back against the wall. Something whizzed past Jacca's head and splattered over the concrete. 'Stupid cakes.'

'I'll come quietly.' He flung his hands in the air and she stared at him in disbelief. 'Let's go inside in case the police come and arrest you for cake murder.'

'You're mad.'

'I'm mad?' He chuckled. 'You're the one tossing defenceless baked goods out of the door!'

'It wouldn't rise and didn't cook properly.'

'And that's the fault of the poor cake?'

'The how-to video promised it would work.' Kaley sounded exasperated.

'What was it supposed to be?'

'A Genoise sponge.'

She had attempted one of the hardest recipes that even professionals chefs often messed up.

'Have you done much baking before?'

The colour rose in her cheeks.

'Define 'much'.'

'Any?'

'Do brownies made from a box mix count?'

'Um, not really. Let's put it this way — I use e-mail and know the basics of Facebook and Twitter but that doesn't make me a computer expert.' He explained the intricacies of a Genoise sponge and the pitfalls of making the light fat-free cake. 'Even the level of humidity in the air makes a difference.'

'A bit like your hair.' She pointed to his unruly mop.

'I thought all women swooned over a tousled mane?' Jacca pretended to be offended. 'It's a trademark of every pirate.'

'Including Red Hawk?' Her challenging dark eyes sucked the breath from him. 'The Michelin-starred pastry chef.'

Busted.

An Unwelcome Visitor

'Do you make a habit of baking for all the cafés you come across in your travels?' Kaley tried to pin him down. 'Is it all part of Red Hawk's carefully cultivated image?'

'Yep. All part of it.' Had she seriously expected him to admit he made the cupcakes because he fancied her? 'Did I say something out of line?'

'No, I'm tired. It's been a long day.'

'If you need my help I'm free tonight.' A cheeky smile tugged at his mouth. 'Tomorrow I go back to charging my usual hourly rates.'

'You won't get any publicity out of this.'

'I don't expect any.' Jacca's quiet response unsettled her. 'Would it be OK if I mixed up a few dozen muffins and cookies?'

'I suppose. You'd better come in.'

Jacca followed her into the kitchen.

'Do you want my help?' she asked.

'Honestly?' He pointed to the trail of cake strewn across the blue tiled floor. 'It'll be safer if you sit down and watch how it's done.'

A wave of exhaustion engulfed her and Kaley steadied herself against the counter.

'Have you eaten? You look about to fall over.' Without waiting for an answer he whisked a frying pan from under the counter and set it on the stove top then turned on the gas with enviable efficiency.

Jacca shrugged off his black coat and rolled up his white shirt sleeves.

'Will a ham and cheese omelette do the trick?'

'That sounds great.' Kaley collapsed into the nearest chair and next thing a mug of coffee appeared on the table in front of her, along with a knife and fork. 'Thanks.'

'No probs.'

The wonderful aroma filling the air stirred her appetite.

'There you go. Enjoy.'

The light gold puffy omelette was a work of art.

'Wow. This looks amazing. Would you mind passing me the pepper?'

'Taste it first. The seasoning should be spot on.'

'Do you bully all your customers or am I today's lucky nominee?' Her challenge kicked his blush-o-meter off the scale again.

'Sorry.' Sandy would smack him around the head. His friend always called him out if he verged into diva territory.

He offered her the pepper mill.

'There you go. I'll get on with baking.' It was too late in the day for anything time-consuming so he'd stick with recipes that held up well overnight or would reheat easily in the morning.

A variety of scones, an orange cinnamon cake and perhaps banana date muffins. Along with several types of cookies she should survive tomorrow. And after that? You can't come back each day and she can't bake. Apart from his growing attraction to Kaley he couldn't

28

help feeling sorry for her.

'That was fantastic.' She pushed away her empty plate. 'Could you teach me how to make that?'

'Before or after our 'Baking for Dummies' lesson?'

'Better make it before. You might be too exasperated to tell me afterwards.'

Her husky laughter settled in the pit of his stomach and he struggled to string his thoughts together.

'For the omelette fold stiff egg whites into your beaten yolks. Always cook it in butter. When it's almost set, sprinkle grated cheese, preferably Gruyere, and diced ham over one half. Fold it over and garnish with julienned basil before serving.'

Out of the blue the back door opened and the last person he expected to see strolled in as though he owned the place.

'I hear you're in need of some help, Kaleisha, honey. Don't worry, your favourite baker has come to the rescue.'

Kaley could happily swing for her mother. Ever since Kaley turned down

Cash Harrison's proposal eight years ago Lorna still mentioned him at regular intervals. She would slip in the fact he hadn't ever married and wonder out loud if like most people he regretted his youthful misbehaviours.

'Do you two know each other?' The elite ranks of computer programmers were a tight-knit group so presumably things were the same with top chefs.

'We've met at a few competitions.' Cash's smile stayed well away from his pale grey eyes. The strange expressions pinging back and forth between the two men set off alarm bells in her head.

'It's all right, Hawken, you can leave me to take care of things now.'

Her anger escalated. She glared at Cash.

'Excuse me but this is none of your business.'

'You'll always be my business.' Cash's cloying musk cologne irritated her nostrils. 'Would you prefer me to go?' Jacca's quiet offer soothed some of her irritation.

'No. He's leaving.'

Cash bridled.

'You're being . . .'

'Stubborn? That was always your favourite complaint about me.' She never understood why he started to pursue her at college until she discovered one of his fraternity brothers dared him to ask her out on a date.

The ultra-conservative Harrison family were polite when Cash introduced her to them but his mother couldn't hide her relief when they broke up.

The man in front of her now was a more solid version of his twenty-one-year-old self with his slicked back ebony hair, grey cashmere coat and polished black dress shoes. Kaley dredged up some manners.

'I appreciate you taking the time to stop by but I'm managing just fine, thank you.'

'Pity. Remember I'll always be there for you.' His voice turned to gravel. 'Call me any time.'

She nodded and watched him leave.

'So, are you going to volunteer what all that was about or do I have to drag it out of you?' Kaley rounded on Jacca.

'It's late and we haven't baked a single muffin yet.' He didn't want to do this now. Truthfully, he didn't want to do it at all. 'I'll do a deal.'

'You'll do a deal?'

'I'll answer your questions tomorrow over dinner and if you're not satisfied you can make me walk the plank.'

'It's a seven-hour drive to the ocean and jumping into Radnor Lake doesn't sound very life-threatening.' A trickle of amusement sneaked into her voice.

He noticed the sprinkling of gold in her dark eyes for the first time. The breath caught in his throat.

'You're slacking on the baking front,' she said, bringing him back down to earth. 'I thought we had a deal.'

'We do and I always keep my promises.'

'Yeah, well, we'll see about that.' Kaley sounded sceptical, whether it was personal or not Jacca couldn't decide.

'Baking lesson number one coming up. Wash your hands well and tie back your hair tight. You'll be glad to return to your computers by the time I'm done with you.'

'I can believe that.'

Jacca would make sure she didn't have the time or energy to verbally spar with him.

Several hours later she groaned as he worked on the knotted muscles in her shoulders until they relaxed under his fingers.

'You don't make a bad sous-chef. Do you fancy a permanent job?'

'You must be kidding.' Kaley sounded horrified.

'Being on your feet for four hours straight, bent over countertops designed for short people, takes its toll.' Jacca chuckled. 'And that was equivalent to maybe half a shift. On the bright side we've baked enough for a few days and your freezer is full.

'If you don't have your own car here I could give you a ride home. I'm pretty sure I've got the hang of driving on the right side of the road now.'

'That's not necessary.'

'I'm not happy with you calling a taxi this late.'

'I'm staying in Connie's apartment.' She gestured up over her head. 'Even poor fragile little me can stumble up twelve stairs and collapse into bed.'

He picked up a towel to dry the last cake pan, stacked it neatly on the wire shelves then fixed the sheet of instructions he'd already gone over with her to the fridge.

'Is our dinner tomorrow night still on the menu?'

'I'm not sure.'

'Fair enough. Ring me if you decide to give it a try.' She didn't look up from cleaning the sink so he shrugged on his coat and left her to it.

Too Much Information

'I warned you to get an early night. What time did you crawl into bed?' Sandy grouched. 'We're due at the studio by six for a seven o'clock slot. The make-up people will need a crane to lift the bags under your eyes.'

'There's something I need to tell you.'

'Now?'

'Sorry.' Jacca sighed. 'Cash Harrison got in touch with me when he heard we were coming to Nashville. He's offered me a business proposition.'

Sandy sunk down in the nearest chair and pulled a bar of chocolate from his pocket.

By the time Jacca finished with his explanation Sandy's snack supply was down a tube of Rolos and a packet of Maltesers.

'Surely investing in some dodgy scheme he's planning in some small town no-one's ever heard of, and putting your name to it as executive pastry chef isn't the right way to raise your profile over here?'

'It could be the perfect way in and make us a boat load of money at the same time.'

'Maybe.' Sandy studied him. 'What else?'

Jacca poured out everything about checking out the Butterscotch Bakery, meeting Kaley and coming face to face with Cash.

'Why did Harrison offer to help her if he wants to get his hands on her bakery? I'm guessing Doctor Kaley Robertson is a total babe?'

Jacca hadn't ventured into the past history between her and the other chef although there clearly was one.

'That's nothing to do with it.'

'If you say so.' Sandy pointed to the bathroom. 'Get showered and meet me downstairs.'

'I owe you.'

'You're darn right you do.' He cracked his first smile of the day. 'One day I'll collect.'

Their friendship forged as five-year-olds on the school playground was unshakeable. 'I know you will.' Jacca grinned back.

★ ★ ★

Kaley turned up the volume on the television as Jacca filled the screen, an amped up version of his warm, charming self. The tattered jeans and faded blue jumper had been replaced by a flattering soft moss-green shirt and chocolate brown cord trousers but his feet still flaunted his trademark bright red clogs.

Under the artificial lights his hair shaded from gold to a rich dark red and fell in an artfully dishevelled mess. Jacca's actual words began to sink in.

'I came to Nashville to raise my baking profile but I'm also considering new investment opportunities. One of your well-known local chefs has an interesting plan to revitalise one section of a small town near here.

'I visited a bakery there today and it's struggling to keep its head above water, along with most of the shops in the area. Our guidance and backing could save them.'

Kaley's cheeks burned when he launched into the story of a sick owner whose family were making touching but inept efforts to keep the bakery going.

'Did he mention this place?' John Green stopped work.

She ignored him and jabbed the remote to stop Jacca mid-sentence. If he came anywhere near her again she would strangle the interfering Englishman.

★ ★ ★

The pile of empty crisp packets and chocolate wrappers next to Sandy told Jacca all he needed to know. They had planned out his answers to the questions he expected to be asked before the show started. He had blithely ignored them.

'You've lost your mind.' Sandy glowered. 'Cash Harrison won't be pleased to hear you've been blabbing about his plan.'

'I didn't give any details or name names.'

Sandy pulled a Mars bar out of his stash.

'Your would-be girlfriend won't be thrilled either.'

'She's not my anything and why would she be cross? It's good publicity. They'll be queuing out the door.'

'You tell everyone the Butterscotch Bakery is on its last legs and expect the dishy doctor to be grateful?'

'It came out wrong.' Jacca flopped on the black leather sofa. 'I've got to see her and explain.'

'Put her out of your mind — we've got a full day planned.' Sandy scrolled through the calendar on his phone.

'I can't.'

'I'm not asking. I'm telling. Do you want me to do my job or not?'

'Yes, of course I do.' They were due to meet three of Nashville's top chefs to discuss some level of involvement by Jacca in their various businesses and then wrap up with a radio talk show before starting

39

all over again tomorrow.

'I'll wangle you a free three-hour slot first thing Thursday morning if that will help.'

Jacca snatched at the olive branch.

'Great.'

'At least working with you is never boring.' Sandy gestured towards the mini-bar. 'I think we deserve a beer.'

Jacca considered raising the amount of sugar his friend had consumed today but kept his mouth shut, opened the fridge and tossed a can to Sandy before popping one open for himself.

'Cheers.' A picture of a beautiful, furious Kaley flashed in front of his eyes and Jacca quickly knocked back his beer to blot it out.

★   ★   ★

'What was that ginger-headed Brit jabbering about? Did Cash let you down?' A trail of raindrops dripped off the hem of Lorna's pink flowery raincoat and she yanked down the hood to fluff up her hair. 'Your daddy's fit to be tied and I've had Connie on the phone in tears.'

'I'm sorry.'

'Good heavens, girl, we won't have a customer left at this rate.'

'Keep your voice down, Mama,' Kaley hissed. 'In case you hadn't noticed I've got people waiting to be served.

'The news of our impending demise hasn't affected their desire for coffee. Help me out and we'll talk when it's quiet.'

The curiosity Jacca had stirred up was drawing people in. Go figure.

'If you can cope out here I'll stick some more muffins and scones in to reheat. I've nearly run out.'

'If I can cope?' Lorna bristled.

Kaley muttered an apology and flew off into the kitchen. The full extent of the business's financial problems preyed on her mind.

When she asked her sister a few pertinent questions Connie casually tossed out her account passwords and log in information over the phone before Kaley could mention the words 'identity theft'.

'Do the best to keep track of things and I'll sort it when I get back.'

'Are you nearly done? I've got customers lined up all the way out to the street.' Lorna poked her head around the door.

'Five minutes.' Later she would force her sister to face the music but right now her oven timer was going off and she dared not burn Jacca's precious muffins.

They survived until closing time at three o'clock when her mother locked the door and sank into the nearest chair.

'Talk about being careful what you wish for.' Lorna's weary laugh made Kaley smile. 'I'd better get home to your poor father. Come over to the house when you're done cleaning up and we'll talk.'

A sweep of gratitude rushed through her for this wonderful woman, her mother in every way that mattered.

'Don't be too late.'

'I wouldn't dare.'

'You would if you thought you could get away with it. Put that last slice of coffee cake in a box for your father to taste.'

'Amazing, isn't it?'

'Yeah. If you learn how to make that, the Butterscotch Bakery might survive.'

She's been stupid to think her parents were unaware of Connie's financial problems. They didn't miss much where their children were concerned.

'I'll try.'

'I know you will.' Her mother gave her a hug and disappeared with a cheery wave.

Kaley owed her family everything and would work herself into the ground rather than let them down.

* * *

Why was he trawling the internet for butterscotch-related recipes instead of focusing on the business in hand? This wasn't the time to ease up.

Sandy was no fan of Cash Harrison but neither was Jacca deep down. There was a difference between confident and egotistical and Harrison frequently crossed the line but his business was a huge success so maybe he could live with the man's personality deficit and work with him?

Jacca continued to stare at the screen and settled on Butterscotch Glazed Coffee-Shortbread Bars as the perfect peace offering. He could picture Kaley crunching the espresso bean off the top before licking off the sticky butterscotch glaze and polishing off the buttery short-bread.

'Suit and tie for this one.' Sandy hiked up a skimpy white towel as he emerged from the bathroom. 'We've got a cute female chef to impress.'

'I don't need Helen Black to fancy me.' I'm only interested in one woman and she would happily grind me up and toss me in the muffin batter right now.

Sandy's large round face sagged.

'You take it all for granted, you lucky devil.'

'What?'

'Women falling at your feet.'

Jacca wanted to call him an idiot but they didn't do lies. Women rarely saw past Sandy's dishevelled bulk to the thoughtful, intelligent man underneath.

'I'll go and change.'

'Thanks.'

'What for?'

'We both know if I lost a few kilos, ditched the glasses and got a decent haircut I'd have better luck.'

He couldn't ask Sandy why he was avoiding doing any of those things because there were layers of reasons — good and bad — why they both behaved in certain ways.

'It isn't going to happen in time for tonight though, mate, so I'll leave the gorgeous Helen to you.'

'Is she?'

'According to her Facebook profile. The picture shows her finishing the Nashville marathon last year.' A ruddy glow heated his cheeks. 'Tall, brunette and with legs long enough to give a giraffe a run for its money.'

'Right,' Jacca drawled. 'Let's make sure Ms Black doesn't know what's hit her when the Brits turn up.'

A Sinking Heart

Kaley held the phone away from her ear as Connie continued to yell.

'I didn't tell you how bad things were because Mom and Dad already loaned me money and I didn't want you coming over all superior and offering to bail me out. Anyway someone offered to buy me out yesterday and I'm considering it.'

'But you can't do that after all the hard work you've put in here. I'm sure we can turn things around.'

'We?' Her sister scoffed. 'Since when do you care about what happens in boring small town Franklin? We've barely seen you since you graduated high school.'

Kaley couldn't defend herself because there was more than a kernel of truth in her sister's observations.

'I'm pretty sure I'll end up taking Cash Harrison's offer.'

'Cash?' Kaley's head span. 'Where does he come into this?' Her heart sank when Connie trotted out the details. He would supposedly clear her sister's debts and then employ her to manage the bakery for him. 'You haven't signed anything yet?'

'I'm not dumb. I told him we'd talk when I come back. Let him sweat.'

'Do you have any update on your travel plans?'

Connie chuckled.

'What you really mean is when can you beat feet back to sunny California? About another ten days if you're lucky. Can you hang in that long? I'm sorry things went south with our yummy Brit.'

Kaley considered mentioning that they had customers queued out of the door again this morning but held her tongue.

'Please don't annoy Cash if he stops by again . . . I really need this.'

'Why? Apart from getting rid of your debts are you in any other trouble?'

'Don't you have work to do?' Avoiding life's unpleasant side was one of her sister's less endearing traits. 'It's nothing for you to worry about. 'Drop it. Please. I've got to go. See you soon.'

Kaley suspected that was almost an apology but Connie hung up before she could be certain.

★   ★   ★

'Toss me the car keys.' Jacca shook Sandy's shoulder to drag his attention away from whatever inane reality show he was glued to now.

'What for?'

'Because I want to drive somewhere?'

'The little lady will smash those precious butterscotch bars in your face,' Sandy warned.

'Kaley is no-one's 'little lady' and you're hardly one to talk about riling up women.'

'How was I supposed to know Helen Black doesn't have a sense of humour?'

'You told her nobody rocked skimpy running shorts better than she does. What did you expect?'

'Women are a puzzle if you ask me and

as far as I'm concerned there's always a piece missing,' Sandy growled.

'Car keys?'

'Take them and go make an idiot of yourself.'

'Thanks.' Jacca snatched the keys from Sandy's outstretched hand.

'Remember we're going to the City House at two o'clock tomorrow afternoon which means leaving here around one.' He pointed to the cake box. 'Give me one to test and don't hassle me about eating too much sugar, either. It's my first all day.'

Jacca didn't say a word. He'd noticed Sandy's longing glances when Helen Black wasn't looking.

'Crikey, mate,' Sandy mumbled through a mouthful of shortbread. 'Market these and we'll be millionaires.'

Jacca had tinkered with the recipe and didn't mind admitting the end result was pretty spectacular.

'I've no desire to run a factory. I'm off.'

'Think about it,' Sandy yelled after

him. 'We could both retire.'

And do what? The kitchen was all he knew. Jacca tucked the box under one arm and took off to face Kaley's wrath.

'Knock, knock. Do I need to dodge flying cakes tonight?' He cautiously poked his head around the door.

'What are you doing here?'

'I came with a peace offering.' Jacca held out the large white box. 'You could make butterscotch glazed coffee shortbread bars your signature item. I combined several ideas I found online to come up with the recipe.'

'After your performance yesterday I'm amazed you dare to show your face.'

Jacca scanned the counter where rows of warm fragrant muffins and cookies sat lined up on wire cooling racks.

'Impressive. All your own work?'

'Yes, but I still want you out of here.'

'You took what I said the wrong way.'

'There's a right way?' Her voice rose. 'You told everyone we're having problems and expect me to be grateful?'

'If it's any consolation my manager

tore me off a strip when I finished the show.' Jacca shrugged. 'Try one.' He opened the box to let a waft of sweet temptation fill the air.

'They smell wonderful.'

'I promise they taste even better.'

He watched Kaley bite off the shiny espresso bean and sink her teeth through the glossy sticky butterscotch glaze into the buttery shortbread. Jacca stifled a grin when she practically melted on the spot.

'The butterscotch becomes fudgier when it sits a while so they'll be better the next day.'

'They won't last that long,' she mumbled. 'I hate admitting this but we've been overwhelmed with new customers who are curious to find out how bad we are. They all went away happy because of your baking and I'm desperate to keep them coming back.'

'I'll apologise if you want me to.'

Kaley's plan to kick Jacca out dissolved as his bright blue eyes bored into her.

'Show me what you baked today.'

'What I baked?' She struggled to pull herself back together. 'Blueberry lemon muffins, chocolate chip coconut cookies and dried cherry almond scones.' Kaley couldn't disguise her pride. 'My true expertise is in computer science so feel free to critique my technique.' Laughter lines fanned around his eyes and the corners of his mouth twitched with amusement. 'Don't say it.'

'I wouldn't dare.' Jacca selected a muffin, broke it apart and examined the inside before taking a bite. 'Next time use fresh blueberries as opposed to dried and double the amount of lemon rind. Meyer lemons are expensive but they're worth it because they give a deeper flavour.'

Next he picked up a cookie.

'Refrigerate the dough longer so they won't fall flat when they're baked and reserve extra chocolate to dot around the top just before they go in the oven. It improves their appearance and more chocolate is always a good thing.'

'At last we agree on something.' Her sly

comment drew out his tantalising smile but it disappeared when he reached for a scone.

'Why do Americans make triangular scones? A proper scone should be round.' He broke one in half and sniffed before tasting. 'Not bad.'

Kaley guessed that on the Red Hawk scale of judging it ranked as at least 'Good' if not 'Very Good'.

'Try plumping up the cherries in hot water first and toast the almonds to ramp up the flavour. Take the scones out of the oven a minute earlier next time, too.' He glanced up and a tinge of colour brightened his pale skin. 'You did ask.'

'Did I complain?'

'Your eyes did the job for you.'

'Sorry, I don't mean to be sensitive.' Kaley sighed. 'I routinely tolerate my programming work being torn apart for a macro that fails but this feels different.'

'I'm taking you out for dinner.'

'Excuse me? Why?'

'Because I'm starving and I bet you haven't eaten either.'

'If you help me clear up the kitchen I'll let you feed me. I want to hear about the man underneath the Red Hawk image.'

All she knew so far of his life path was the carefully constructed image he projected on social media. The only son of a single mother from a remote part of England he was initially self-taught before he attended culinary school in Paris.

After working his way up the ladder he regularly swept the awards at international pastry competitions, had written a cookery book considered by many to be the pastry chef's bible and along the way acquired the nickname Red Hawk because of his flaming hair and fierce work ethic.

'Be careful what you ask for.' A touch of sadness crept into his voice and he moved towards the counter. He began to stack cookies in plastic boxes and she joined in. 'Just so you know I'm not rushing back to England next week.'

Kaley didn't ask why he needed to tell her that.

'Good.'

Neither of them mentioned the following days, weeks and months.

'If we don't put the scones away soon they'll dry out and I can't be responsible for their demise because it's against the pirate chef code.' He chuckled. 'Article six amendment thirteen.'

'In that case let's save the scones from certain death.'

Kaley pushed away her doubts and worries, including the newest addition — an e-mail sent by her boss sent hours ago which she hadn't yet found the nerve to read. The message was labelled High Importance and she doubted it was the good news.

A New Image

'Now I've seen it all.' Jacca strolled into the hotel gym and tossed his towel on the treadmill next to Sandy. Red-faced and dripping with sweat his friend was lumbering away as though his life depended on it.

'I thought you were still sleeping. You must be mad to do this every day.'

It wasn't hard to guess Helen Black was the reason behind this sudden about-face.

'You need to build up slowly.' Otherwise you'll kill yourself because the last time you ventured near a gym Tony Blair was Prime Minister.

'I don't get why people enjoy this.' Sandy turned the machine off and grabbed his water bottle, draining it in one long swallow.

'Most don't.' Jacca set the speed on his own treadmill. 'I work out so I can eat without getting . . .'

'Flabby?' Sandy jiggled his stomach.

'Blame my mother's cooking and my own greed. Your cakes don't help.'

'I'll quit offering them.'

'Get real,' Sandy grumbled. 'What difference will it make? Helen Black is convinced I'm a dinosaur. The weight's irrelevant.'

'Ignore her, then, and do it for the sake of your health. How many people in your family — '

'I didn't ask for a lecture.' He guzzled down a second bottle of water. 'I didn't hear you come in last night?'

'You were snoring like a pig.' Jacca laughed. 'I took Kaley out for dinner after we finished at the bakery.'

He wasn't going into details about the long conversation they had over their meal.

She had started by explaining she was the result of a holiday romance between a Norwegian Olympic gold medal skier and a Jamaican nurse but that her parents split up after her birth. She ended up being shunted around various Jamaican relatives until one of her aunts brought her to the United States.

'I've got vague memories of my aunt Delyse but she died in a car crash when I was only three and I ended up in foster care,' she'd told him.

Lorna and Spencer Robertson already had their toddler daughter Connie but their plan to have another biological child changed when they visited a local children's home one Christmas and met the skinny four-year-old with huge brown eyes. They hadn't been able to resist Kaley.

'That's my story, what's yours?' she'd asked.

He'd attempted to make his own childhood sound less grim but suspected she saw beneath his fake cheerfulness.

'Is it wise to get close to her under the circumstances?' Sandy asked.

The comment stung. As if he didn't know getting involved with Kaley was a terrible idea. Jacca pointed to the treadmill.

'You were right. It'll take more than this to impress Helen.'

'Thanks for the support, mate. You've got an hour before we leave for Franklin. Manny Marshall at Sweet Treats wants to meet you.' Sandy slung his sweaty towel around his shoulders. 'There won't be time for a detour to your girlfriend's place, either.'

'But you promised me a free morning. I told Kaley I'd be there.'

'Tough. I'm doing my job.'

Sandy barrelled out of the room. Jacca turned up the speed and pounded the treadmill into submission.

★ ★ ★

Kaley stepped out of the back door and allowed the raw January day to work its magic on her overheated face. She pulled out her phone and found another message from her boss.

'War of World Play project critical. I need your input now. If that's not possible we must discuss alternatives.'

This coveted job would slide Bao Chang's way. The hard-charging MIT grad was Kaley's assistant and he'd made no secret of his ambition to snatch the top job away from her at the first opportunity.

Kaley bit the bullet and returned the call. Five minutes later she had promised to return when Connie was fit enough to run the bakery again but had been given no guarantee about what job she'd go back to.

Jacca's words popped into her head: 'Just so you know I'm not rushing back to England next week.'

Over dinner last night at Kayne Prime, one of Nashville's top steakhouses, she got a small measure of Jacca's contradictions.

On the surface he was an easy-going man with a wry sense of humour but peel back a layer and a very different man emerged, confident in his culinary skills and serious about spreading the Red Hawk brand worldwide.

Still at his core, though, was an insecure boy. Jacca gave himself away the most when he spoke about his oldest friend and business manager. He would do anything for Alessandro Vitale and the same was true in reverse.

'Taking a break?'

'Oh, it's you.'

'I've had more enthusiastic welcomes.' Jacca tilted a questioning glance her way. 'What's a man got to do for a decent smile these days?'

'Make three orange coffee cakes for tomorrow? You're late.'

'I shouldn't even be here. Sandy will string me up for bailing on him. We had a bit of a set-to and I said a few things I regret about his weight and . . . stuff.'

She brushed a thick springy curl back away from his face.

'Sweet Treats is only a five-minute walk from here and you can say you lost your way . . . that wouldn't be far wrong, would it?'

'No.' He sighed. 'I'll be the perfect client for once. After we're through with the business side of things I'll put the rest right. At least I hope so.'

'Call me.' Kaley almost shared the

mixed news about her job but there were things she needed to sort out in her own mind first.

'Go back in and sell cakes.' He gave her a playful push back towards the door and despite everything she couldn't help giggling.

* * *

'I didn't expect you to turn up.' Sandy tapped his watch. 'We're five minutes late.'

'I'll explain it's my fault. I see business is good.' A queue of people stretched out of the door and halfway down the street. A ruddy faced man grabbed him by the shoulder when Jacca edged on around.

'Where do you think you're goin', buddy?'

'We've got a meeting with Manny.' Sandy loomed over the stranger and treated him to what Jacca called his Mafia stare. 'No hassle, eh?'

It was a struggle not to laugh when the man turned pale and stepped out of the way.

As soon as they went in the door he recognised Manny Marshall working his way around the tables and chatting to his customers. His booming laughter was incongruous coming from the tiny dapper man wearing his trademark white linen suit and red polka dot bow tie.

Jacca slipped back into Red Hawk mode and went to work. An hour later they had a verbal agreement to join Manny and two other local pastry chefs in a top billing slot at the upcoming Music City Food Festival.

'What's next?' He hardly dared to ask Sandy for the tedious details but gave himself a mental kick for thinking about it that way.

'A radio show at five followed by a cocktail reception at the Country Music Hall of Fame. That's a charity fundraiser catered by several of the big hotels and you'll need to work the charming red-headed Brit angle to the max there.'

'How about a quick beer? There's an Irish bar called McClosky's a couple of streets over.'

'All right, but you're buying and don't walk too fast, either — my legs are killing me from that stupid treadmill.'

'You'll notice a difference in a week or two.'

Sandy shook his head.

'Yes, being six feet under should be a great painkiller.'

They laughed and strolled along together. He must be getting absent-minded in his old age because he'd somehow forgotten to mention the bar was close to the Butterscotch Bakery. Odd, that.

Mutual Interest

Kaley daydreamed with the cleaning rag in her hand. Weren't holiday romances usually conducted on white sandy beaches while sipping fruity drinks decorated with paper umbrellas? Damp, chilly Franklin in the middle of January wouldn't strike most people as an enticing setting but thinking about Jacca made the blood flow faster through her veins.

It only took a quick glance around the empty shop to toss cold water on her idle thoughts. Most of Connie's regular customers were gone by late morning and business continued to decline steadily until they closed at three.

Jacca would notice a huge difference over at Manny Marshall's café. Admittedly Connie wasn't as well-known but location played a huge part of the Sweet Treat bakery's success.

She reached for her notepad and pen, a habit she'd never abandoned from her school days that always made her techie colleagues roar with laughter.

It was clear they needed to find their niche market. Perhaps if they widened their options to include a few simple cooked dishes and kept to the same menu all day they could make breakfast at the Butterscotch Bakery the thing to do? The real question was how to pull off this miracle when the whole Dixie Street area was struggling?

Kaley decided to carry out an unscientific survey on her last remaining customer. She poured two cups of coffee and selected a couple of cherry almond scones that weren't likely to sell now.

'Do you mind if I join you for a few minutes?' She treated John Green to her brightest smile. 'My feet are killing me and I need to pick your brains.'

His deep grey eyes widened.

'Did you sample one of my new scones?' They both knew he never bought anything to eat and made a single cup of coffee last for hours.

'Um . . . no.'

'They're dried cranberry and almond and there's a fresh coffee for you, too.'

'Thanks.' He still looked wary.

'Why do you come here?'

'Is this a trick question?'

'No.' Give me strength. 'I mean why do you come here as opposed to any other café in Franklin?' Apart from the fact that my gullible sister doesn't pester you to move on, she added silently.

'It's close to my apartment.'

'That's it?'

'Yeah, pretty much.'

'Do you talk to any of the other customers?'

'Talk?' His doctorate from the Massachusetts Institute of Technology plainly hadn't covered social skills.

'Forget it.' Kaley sighed. 'I'm sorry I bothered you.'

'No, I'm sorry.' A shock of pale blond hair flopped over his forehead. 'I'm out of the habit of .. interacting with people.'

'Oh, I totally get that. I'm a computer person, too.'

'Really?'

Kaley couldn't blame him for sounding dubious and ran through her professional résumé.

'Don't worry about it.' She explained what she was trying to achieve. 'I'm afraid as the only customer you've got stuck with my ramblings.'

'I occasionally overhear conversations going on around me and . . . I hate saying this but before you tried out a few new recipes people often said the food was dull.'

'I can see where they're coming from.'

'You can?'

Kaley grinned.

'Yeah, but don't tell my sister.'

'I wouldn't dream of it,' John stammered. 'She's such a kind person.'

OMG. He must fancy Connie. Who would've guessed it?

'I need you to be honest.' She fished out her notebook.

'It's the only way I know how to be.'

'Good, now listen to these ideas I've come up with.'

'You've got twenty minutes max with your lady.' Sandy warned. 'The taxi's picking us up at four.' They'd decided not to drive themselves and risk the chance of getting lost and being late for their various appointments.

'Come with me and meet Kaley.'

'Are you sure?'

A retraction hovered on the end of his tongue but Jacca didn't want to rattle the fragile peace they'd arrived at after a couple of beers.

'Of course I am.' This time as they walked along he sized up Dixie Street more closely. Several of the houses were still private residences but the rest were small businesses including an estate agent, a lawyer, a music studio and a hairdresser.

'It's a bit out of the way and there isn't much foot traffic.'

'Don't you think Harrison's plan to stick up a hotel and swanky restaurant out here is crazy?'

'Perhaps but I've done my homework and Cash isn't spinning me a line when he says Franklin is experiencing a resurgence. Property values are soaring but this section of the city is still reasonably priced.'

Sandy's eyes narrowed.

'Kaley will have your guts for garters if she finds out you only came here initially to scope out the lay of the land. Did Cash encourage you to turn on the Red Hawk charm so she'd encourage her sister to sell it cheap?'

'No — in fact he wasn't happy to see me out here.' Jacca tried to defend himself. Harrison might have planned to use his own long-standing relationship with Kaley but that was pure speculation.

Sandy grimaced at the rectangular blue and white sign over the bakery door.

'Very nondescript. Unless you know it's there you'd walk right by.'

Jacca pushed open the door and strode in.

'Yo ho, your favourite pirate is here.'

Kaley was engrossed in conversation

with the same customer he'd spoken to the other day.

'Oh, I didn't expect to see you.' A flicker of guilt shot across her face as she jumped up. 'You must be Sandy.'

'Whatever story he told you, don't believe a word.'

'Isn't it your job to bolster your clients' reputation?' Jacca laughed.

'Yes, but that's a challenge when I've known you since you were a snotty-nosed five-year-old.'

'I can imagine.' He turned to Kaley. 'Did we interrupt you in the middle of something?' His question brought a tinge of colour to her dark skin.

'Just computer talk. Nothing important.'

'I ought to be off.' John Green packed away his laptop.

'Don't leave on our account. We can't stay long.'

'I was going anyway. I'll see you tomorrow.' Green nodded at Kaley who gave him a tight-lipped smile.

'Can I get you guys anything?' You

guys? Jacca resented being treated like any another customer.

'No, thanks. We've got a taxi coming in a few minutes. I'd like to take a look around, if you don't mind?' Sandy wandered over to the counter without waiting for a reply.

Kaley and Jacca stood there staring at each other and neither of them spoke.

'This man's got to get off to work or we'll both be in the poor house.' Sandy cleared his throat next to them. 'I'll wait outside. You've got two minutes. Sorry, but he pays me well to ruin his life.'

Jacca almost followed his friend out, swept by a rare sense of uncertainty.

'You know I can't stop now, Kaley.' He lowered his voice. 'I'll ring you later to find out the truth on Nerd Boy. I'm not idiotic enough to have the wrong idea about the pair of you but you're up to something.' Her cheeks heated.

'One question before I run off. Where do I stand with you?' That wasn't at all what he intended to ask but it popped out before he could censor himself. 'If you're still involved with Cash Harrison I'd rather know now.'

'I'm not. He's part of my past.'

'Does he know that?'

'He should. I've given him no encouragement since I turned down his proposal the day we graduated from college.'

'Good.' He lifted his hand to touch her soft cheek. 'Later.' Later couldn't come soon enough.

The Kiss That Never Happened

'Somebody should have told us 'Casual Dress' meant cowboy boots and hats.'

Sandy popped another canapé in his mouth.

'Bit unexpected, isn't it?' They were either overdressed or underdressed depending how their fellow guests looked at it.

'I see the British invasion is trundling along.' Helen Black's orange silk dress was definitely eye-catching and Jacca could tell she knew it. 'Come with me. Nico wants to meet you both.' She ran her sparkling emerald eyes over Sandy. 'No boots and hat required.'

Helen slipped her hand through the crook of Sandy's arm and treated him to a brilliant smile while Jacca trailed along behind.

'This is Nico Chastain, my boss.'

'Boss? Who's she kidding?' The

rail-thin man's blond wavy hair, black sequinned suit and silver-heeled boots meant he'd never go unnoticed even in this crowd. 'Everyone knows who runs the sweet side of Chastain Enterprises and it sure ain't me.' He sized up Jacca. 'She tells me you're the real deal and we oughta snatch you up.'

He couldn't hide his surprise.

'Is there any chance we could meet privately when this shindig winds down?' Sandy suggested.

'Sure. The Barlines sports bar in the Omni hotel is a five-minute walk from here. They do killer wings and a Moon-shine cheeseburger that drips down your face.'

'You had us at wings and reeled us in with cheeseburgers.'

'Do I get an invite or have I served my purpose?' Helen sounded offended but Jacca suspected it was an act.

'When I said 'we' I naturally meant all of us.' Sandy stumbled over his words.

'She's teasing you, buddy.' When Nico winked and clasped his friend's shoulder another trickle of disquiet ran through him.

'Oh, right. We'll catch you later.'

Jacca spotted Cash heading their way but couldn't see any way to escape coming face to face.

'We need a word, Hawken.'

Next thing he found himself steered over to a corner of the large room.

'What's up?'

'From now on you steer clear of the Butterscotch Bakery.'

'Why?'

'Don't play dumb with me. Ms Robertson won't need your so-called help when I buy the place from her sister.' He gripped Jacca's arm. 'Kaley doesn't come as part of the Dixieside development scheme.'

'She gave me the impression the two of you are ancient history.'

'That's an impression I intend to correct and I'm pretty sure she won't object — so keep your hands off her.' Harrison's gaze swept over Sandy. 'A word of advice.' A smirk played around his thin lips. 'Helen Black is way out of your league. You'll have better luck working your fancy English accent on some of the celebrity hangers-on here tonight. They aren't as fussy.'

Jacca tugged on his friend's arm.

'Let's go.' For a second Sandy didn't move but then he pushed off through the crowd.

'I can't believe you're seriously considering going into business with that idiot.'

'Come on, we both know you've had it in for him ever since Vienna.'

'Wake up and smell the roses, Jax, it was obvious he cheated in that competition.' Sandy's frustration erupted.

'The judges couldn't prove it.' Growing up, he was looked down on by people who didn't know his full story and tried to make a point now of never doing the same to anyone else. If he sometimes leaned too far the other way, surely that wasn't a bad thing?

'The fact he's still carrying a torch for a woman he once loved isn't necessarily a red flag. I might try to warn off another man if the boot was on the other foot. It doesn't mean we can't do business together.' Deep in his gut Jacca wasn't sure he believed what he was saying.

'I give in.' Sandy flung up his hands in surrender. 'Let's circulate.'

★ ★ ★

Kaley yawned and stretched out on the bed. If Jacca didn't call soon she would be a bleary-eyed mess in the morning. All of a sudden her phone gave an annoying beep.

'Sorry. Got delayed. Will be in touch tomorrow. Sleep well.'

Kaley turned it off without responding. Let him believe she went to bed without caring if they spoke. John Green's question kept on reverberating in her head.

'Haven't you heard the rumours? Two of the houses along this street were snatched up as soon as they went on sale and they say someone's planning to tear all of Dixie Street down to build a boutique hotel with a fancy restaurant.'

She fired her laptop back up and after slogging through pages and pages of information her eyes burned with exhaustion. Anger simmered barely under the surface as she reached for the phone to ring her sister.

'I hope you're going to ask what on earth I'm talking about. Please say Cash didn't tell you about this proposed hotel development? It'll destroy the whole area.'

'Good morning to you, too,' Connie chirped. 'Don't I get the usual 'How's your leg and when are you coming home?' questions today?'

'No.' Kaley rattled off the details of her conversation with John Green and the results of her online research.

'I need the money.' Connie's sigh travelled down the line.

'You can't be so desperate for money you're willing to let the bakery be destroyed?'

'I'm not. Mom and Dad are.'

A loud silence filled the distance

between them. Their parents lived modestly and had used the compensation payment from Spencer's accident to pay off their mortgage.

'Why?' Kaley's heart froze as her sister poured out the whole sad story. A new experimental treatment might help their father with the chronic pain that dominated his life but the expensive drug wasn't covered by his medical insurance.

'But Cash isn't offering you a fair price.'

'The development hasn't been approved yet so he's taking a chance.'

Kaley said nothing. It didn't take a genius to guess her ex had an inside track on the plans.

'The doctor warned that if Dad doesn't start the drug within the next month he won't be strong enough to tolerate the side effects. I'm not happy about the redevelopment plans but Dad comes first.'

Kaley took a couple of steadying breaths.

'What can I do?'

'Thank you.'

'What for?'

'Trusting me. I've sweet talked my doctor into letting me fly back on Monday and he convinced the airline into upgrading me to business class to accommodate my leg. Try not to run my business into the ground before then.'

Kaley slumped back on the bed and two hours later her alarm went off again.

* * *

Jacca screwed up his bleary eyes against the light streaming in through the sheer white curtains.

'Get out of bed and shower ASAP.' Sandy loomed into view, fully dressed and with a face like thunder.

'What's the hurry?'

'We're meeting with the festival committee to secure our spot. Non-negotiable.'

'I'm struggling to put together what happened last night.' The night had disappeared in a haze of exhaustion. 'Did we sign anything? Promise to hand over our first born children?'

'No, but we made a verbal agreement for you to do three guest pastry chef gigs in Chastain's restaurant group over the next year.'

'You sure?'

'Every minute is engraved on my brain.' Sandy vowed. 'I wish most of them weren't.'

Slivers of memory were returning, few of them good.

'How much time do I have?'

'Fifteen minutes until we leave here and then I'll be grilling you in the taxi on what we're going to say. There's no time to call Kaley. I'm going to eat my waffles and bacon while you get ready. Do you want me to save you some?'

Jacca shuddered.

'Black coffee will do.'

'I've got to keep my strength up.' Sandy patted his stomach.

'I thought you were heartbroken?' Jacca wished he hadn't been proved right. Helen had flirted relentlessly with his friend then taken great pleasure in turning him down.

'I'm better on my own and might as well get used to it.' A fleeting shadow dimmed his smile. 'They need to see Red Hawk at his best.' Sandy made a swipe at Jacca's stubbly jaw. 'Ed Sheeran and Prince Harry might get away with it but you resemble a derelict.'

'Cheers.' Jacca cleared off to the bathroom and turned on the shower to cover up the sound of the phone he'd sneaked in.

'Don't hang up on me,' he begged Kaley. 'I can't talk long because I'm supposed to be showering. It's a long story but it turned into a late night and now we're off to a meeting. I'll be free by around five o'clock.'

'Pick me up at six and feed me then I'll consider forgiving you.'

'That's a date.' He ended the call with the ghost of a smile on his face.

★ ★ ★

Jacca slipped in the hotel key card and pushed back the door with one foot.

'Check out the awesome view.'

Kaley wandered over to stare out of the large expanse of windows where downtown Nashville sparkled beneath them in the fading light.

'I love the edgy vibe of a city.' She smiled at him. 'No red clogs tonight?' He'd abandoned his usual casual wear for pale grey slacks, a dark blue shirt and polished black loafers.

'It's good to change things up sometimes. Would you like a glass of champagne before I have to leave you for about ten minutes?'

'Leave? Aren't we going out to eat?'

'No. I've got a surprise for you.' He popped the cork on the champagne and poured her a glass.

Kaley took a sip then flopped down on the soft white leather couch and kicked off her shoes.

'How you do this day in and day out I'll never know.'

'It gets in your blood.' What else could

a chef do to impress a woman but cook for her? He prepared their meal in the hotel kitchen earlier and it should only take him about five minutes to pull it together now. 'I won't be long.'

Jacca tapped on the door before pushing the loaded trolley in and let out a sigh at the sight of Kaley sprawled out fast asleep. He crept across to tuck a pillow under her head and as he lifted up a handful of her thick hair a drift of her spicy hibiscus shampoo wafted his way. He made a quick retreat to the other side of the room and slumped in a chair by the window.

'Wow, we're a hopeless pair. This is a super exciting date.'

He jerked upright and rubbed his eyes. 'We both slept?'

'I guess so. It's nine o'clock and my stomach is growling, I don't know about yours.'

'I cooked dinner for us.' He pointed at the trolley and rattled off the menu — a lemon and dill shrimp appetiser followed by filet mignon and a tropical mille-feuille. 'I can salvage the appetiser and dessert because they're both served cold but the steaks are ruined.'

'There's a microwave over there on the counter. Nuke them.'

She wanted him to cremate 200 dollars' worth of Japanese Kobe steaks?

'Are you trying to get back in my good books or not?'

'We'll start with the shrimp.' He whisked the lid off the appetiser plates.

'That's a shame, I'm allergic to shell-fish.'

'Oh, sorry . . . I never thought to ask.'

'Got you! It's fun to tease you for a change.' Kaley popped a shrimp in her mouth. 'That's delicious.'

He almost said, 'So are you' but felt unaccountably nervous around her tonight. Maybe she wasn't interested. Perhaps Cash Harrison was right and she still held a candle for him? The business implications were there too, hanging around like a hungry buzzard.

Kaley glanced down at her empty plate.

'What's next?'

Jacca obediently reheated the steaks, dauphinoise potatoes and grilled asparagus.

'Just remember . . . '

'You're better than this. Yeah, I get it.' She grinned and Jacca couldn't help smiling back.

Their eyes locked and as they leaned into each other Kaley's heart raced. Instead of kissing her, Jacca shifted back in the chair and his smile faded.

'I bumped into Cash at a charity do last night and . . . he warned me off seeing you again. He told me he wants to get back together with you and thinks you want the same thing.'

'Well, he's wrong. Please tell me you're not going to take any notice.'

He hesitated for a moment.

'I certainly don't want to but Harrison is hugely influential locally and could wreck my chance of breaking into the Nashville culinary scene. I really care for you . . . '

'But not enough.' She pushed her

plate away. 'It's late and I need to get some sleep before the alarm clock goes off again.'

'Don't leave this way.'

'Which way would you like me to go? Down the fire escape? ?'

'Kaley, I never meant to upset you. How will you manage the bakery . . . '

'Without the esteemed Red Hawk holding my hand? Don't worry about me.' She grabbed her coat and rushed out before he could change her mind. Outside the hotel she slowed down to pull out her phone and call for a ride home.

Had she been too hard on him? Jacca's desire to prove himself was the same she saw reflected back in the mirror every morning.

Recently the realisation had trickled in that being there for the people who'd loved and supported her meant more than pushing for the next big success on her upward career path. Unless he felt the same way there could never be any future for them.

If she went straight to the bakery now maybe she could push Jacca and the kiss that didn't happen from her mind.

A Safe Bet?

Kaley smiled when her sister appeared being pushed in a wheelchair by a handsome pilot.

'Give me a hug.'

Their disagreements didn't matter now. Her sister was home safe.

'Are you sure you can manage, ma'am?' The pilot frowned. 'I'd be happy to help you get this sweet little girl to your car.'

'We're fine but thanks for your help.' Kaley took the wheelchair. 'And you can stop pouting.'

'You're mean.' Connie sighed. 'Isn't Russ cute?' She chattered on about meeting the pilot when he left the cockpit for a break. 'He sat down to talk because I looked so forlorn.'

Forlorn? You've never been forlorn in your life, Kaley thought.

'Let's get going, it's rush hour.'

Connie slumped back in the wheelchair and sulked while they made their way to the car and headed out of the airport.

'Get off at the Moores Lane exit and pull into the Sonic. I'm dying for a greasy burger and tater tots. Add an order of onion rings too.'

'Plus a cherry limeade with extra cherries, I suppose.' Her sister adored the Fifties-style burger joint with its roller-skating carhops and retro menu.

'You're the best and I know that's not what I said the other day.' Connie's eyes filled with tears.

'It's OK, you're tired and I'm sure you're sick of dealing with that.' She pointed to the plaster cast. 'We'll talk tomorrow. Let's get you some food. If you can't make it up the stairs later you'll have to sleep at Mom and Dad's.'

'No way. I'm looking forward to being in my own bed if I have to crawl there. But where are you gonna sleep?'

'On the couch.' Kaley kept to herself how little sleep she'd survived on while trying to keep the Butterscotch Bakery afloat. 'I told our folks we'll go over for dinner tomorrow when you've revived a bit. Why don't you give them a call now before you flake out?'

'Yes, ma'am.' Connie gave a fake salute. 'You're still as bossy as ever.'

'And you're still stroppy.' But we'll always be sisters. Blood has nothing to do with it.

* * *

'You idiot.' Sandy shook his head. 'You basically told Kaley she's less important to you than making money.'

'Maybe, but we came here to build up my brand and Cash Harrison is a big cheese in the Nashville culinary scene whether we like it or not.'

'Does making it in America really matter?'

It had half killed him to watch Kaley's eyes flood with disappointment when he didn't kiss her.

But from day one in the kitchen Jacca had focused all of his talent and drive on proving himself to his mother in an effort to make up for his father's desertion.

Ethel always told him how Rob Hawken had complained about being neglected in favour of his baby son.

'Think about it, mate.' Sandy clapped a hand on his shoulder. 'This is it. You ready?' He checked his watch again as they climbed out of the taxi.

Of all the people slated for receiving the Red Hawk charm treatment today this was the one Jacca had been dreading the most. Cash Harrison's the Cracked Biscuit restaurant on the top floor of the luxurious hotel was considered a benchmark for upscale Southern cuisine but according to Nico Chastain the man wasn't well liked.

No great surprise there. He'd also picked up the general impression that Harrison's excellent staff carried the restaurant's reputation on their backs.

'You should've joined the army.'

'You pay me to get you where you're supposed to be when you're supposed to be there.' Sandy took their business relationship seriously.

'I know and I appreciate it, even if I

don't often say so.'

Three o'clock in the afternoon was the slack time between lunch and dinner. With no customers to serve the staff got all the prep work done for the evening then and then ate an early meal together.

As soon as they stepped out of the lift Cash flung open the restaurant's front doors.

'Welcome to my corner of the world.' Jacca was thrown by his affable manner. 'I hope you'll join us to eat.'

'We couldn't possibly trouble you.'

'It's no trouble. There's always plenty of food.'

They spent an hour talking shop and sampling a wide selection of superb Mexican dishes prepared by one of the line cooks, before Harrison showed them into his office and switched the conversation to the possible investment deal.

'Why exactly do you want to get me involved?' Sandy's dubiousness was rubbing off on Jacca.

'You're a great pastry chef and a shrewd businessman.' Cash's smile appeared forced. 'We wouldn't need you here full time. You put together the dessert menu and train my staff to fulfil your vision then leave me to take care of the rest.

'Within five years Dixieside will rival the French Laundry and you'll make a boatload of money for very little work.'

The idea of creating a viable rival to Thomas Keller's renowned restaurant verged on lunatic but he hesitated to say so.

'What will happen to the Butterscotch Bakery?' He needed to hear it spelled out.

'It'll be demolished along with the rest of the street. We both know it'll be bankrupt by the end of the year anyway.'

'That won't endear you to Kaley and the rest of her family.'

'Don't worry about that. I'll win over the little lady and take care of her.' A satisfied smirk crept across Harrison's face.

Big mistake. The 'little lady' didn't need anyone to 'take care' of her. Jacca caught Sandy's faint smile and knew they were thinking along the same lines.

'What are the chances that the project will be approved?'

'I know it will.' Cash tapped the side of his nose. 'It pays to know the right people. My cousin is on the Franklin city council, the mayor's an old friend of my daddy and the head of the Historic Zoning Commission is a fellow BGA graduate.'

Jacca didn't see that razing the area for this proposed development was a stellar idea. Surely bringing it back to life in a similar way to the centre of Franklin would be a far better move?

'I've heard that Connie Robertson is back in town and she's a big fan of yours. You should go over there and butter her up to help out our case.'

Harrison's persistence irritated Jacca.

'There is no 'our case' yet.'

'Don't take too long to decide or someone else will jump in.'

'Don't we need to get to our next appointment?' Jacca nodded over to Sandy.

'We certainly do.'

There was no other appointment but Jacca needed to get out of there — and fast.

'I'll make my decision within a week and thanks again for the great meal.' He'd already personally thanked Luiz Rodriguez.

'You're wavering?' Sandy questioned him the minute they stepped foot outside.

'I'm not convinced the scheme is right for the area plus I'm not sure I could work with Harrison.'

'What about if he wasn't involved and we came up with a less drastic plan?'

'Perhaps.' Jacca wasn't sure what his old friend was getting at.

'Chastain might be interested.'

'Nico? Why would he consider going into business with us?'

'He hinted at a few things the other night. This way you might get Kaley and a deal. Isn't she worth a bit of effort?'

Off the top of his head Jacca couldn't think of a smart response.

'I've seen everything now.' Connie hobbled into the kitchen and eased herself on to one of the stools before resting her crutches up against the counter. 'My fancy PhD sister covered in flour and rolling out scones. How are the mighty fallen.'

After a miserable few hours spent on a lumpy sofa Kaley wasn't in a joking mood.

'How was your night?'

'Lousy. Jet lag and an itchy leg aren't a good combination.'

Kaley slid a tray of scones into the oven.

'What are those?'

'Lavender and lemon curd.' Kaley waited for the axe to fall.

'That's not one of my recipes.'

'I've experimented with a few new things.'

'You? But you know diddly squat about baking.' Connie turned to read the chalk board on the wall. 'You've revamped my whole menu.'

Kaley set the timer and dusted off her hands before taking a deep breath. She explained about Jacca's efforts, her chat with John Green and her tentative efforts to increase the profile of the Butterscotch Bakery.

'You sly weasel.' A wide smile lit up Connie's face. 'When do I get to meet our red-haired saviour?' When she didn't answer immediately her sister homed in with the precision of a guided missile. 'Oh boy. Does he fancy you, too?'

'Of course not. I mean . . .'

'Ha! I knew it.' Connie almost wobbled off the stool in her excitement. 'What happened? I want every detail.'

'I don't have time now — we're late opening up.' Kaley craned her neck to peer out through the café when someone knocked on the door. 'You're about to get your wish.'

'Which one?'

'To meet your baking hero.'

'Red Hawk is here?'

Jacca tried humour as his first weapon. 'Um, excuse me but are you open?

The sign says you are.'

'But there's no smell of freshly baked muffins or fragrant coffee brewing?'

Every time he laid eyes on Kaley her beauty made him catch his breath.

'Don't tell me — today's special is lavender and lemon curd.' He theatrically wrinkled his nose. 'Plus you've mastered the buttermilk, cheddar and apple scones.'

'If you keep that man to yourself one more second I'll swat you.' A bubbly blonde with laughing blue eyes hobbled over on crutches.

'I can't believe Red Hawk is standing in my bakery although I know you've been here before because my sweet sister told me everything.' She dragged at his arm. 'Come in. Open up, Kaley, while I talk to this amazing man.'

'Any other orders?'

The edge to her voice told him Kaley was distinctly unhappy, either with him, her sister or both of them.

'Yeah, when you've got a few spare minutes bring us two coffees and a plate of those new scones. As the owner I should test what's been sneaked on to my menu while I wasn't looking.'

John Green strolled in and set his laptop bag on the usual corner table.

'Kaley, can I have my usual, please, when you've . . . '

'A free minute? Yeah, why not? I've plenty of those.'

'Sorry. I'll come up and fetch it.'

'No, I'm the one who's sorry.' A tired smile played around her dark eyes. 'Sit down and I won't be long. There are two new scones on the menu today.'

'Surprise me.'

'Surprise me?' Connie's voice turned shrill. 'Has the world gone mad? My least adventurous customer who's drunk the same medium roast coffee, heavy on the cream and sugar, for the last three years and never buys anything to eat wants you to surprise him?

'My nerdy sister has turned into a baker and . . . the most phenomenal pastry chef in the whole world has been reinventing my store.' Her eyes shone.

'And stirring up my sister to boot.'

'Have fun.' Kaley fixed him with a sly half-smile. 'Some of us have work to do.'

'No-one's introduced us but you must be the talented Connie.' Jacca turned on the charm. She could be a valuable ally in his attempt to win over her sister.

'Yep, I sure am. Let's sit.' She limped over to the nearest table.

'Let me take those.' He rested her crutches against the wall before pulling up a chair next to her.

'I've read your official bio but it's short on details and I want the whole shebang. Tell me how a boy from some remote part of England ends up as a top pastry chef?'

'Talent.' Jacca felt himself blush. 'That's a rather un-British thing to say but I've a talent for baking. It's no different from being a piano protégé or a natural linguist. But I had help from a lot of other chefs along the way.'

'My sister's the same way about her computers and I swear she'd marry one if it was legal.'

'She's a smart woman.'

'Yeah, and don't you forget it.' Connie's warning made him grimace. He'd underestimated this sister, too.

In an effort to mitigate her earlier rudeness Kaley put one each of today's new scones on a plate, poured out a mug of coffee and set it all down in front of John.

'Thank you. Goodness, I envy him.'

'Who?'

'Wonder Chef.' He nodded towards Jacca. 'I wish I could talk to women as easily.'

'No, what you mean is you wish you could talk to that particular woman. You don't have any trouble chatting to me.'

'That's different.'

'Because you don't fancy me?'

A blotchy rash of heat zoomed up his neck.

'I wouldn't put it that bluntly.'

'Why not? It's the truth.' Kaley shrugged. 'It's OK, I don't mind. You're a nice guy but I don't fancy you, either.'

'You're quite something, you know

that?' John's deep grey eyes sparkled.

Was the idea of pairing her wacky sister with this introverted genius totally off the wall?

'Don't get any ideas,' John added.

'What about?'

'Matchmaking.'

'It never occurred to me.'

'Liar.' He waggled his finger at her. 'I'll do my own, thank you very much.'

Kaley fished a ten-dollar bill out of her pocket and slapped it on the table.

'This says you don't have the nerve to ask Connie out.'

'Give me forty-eight hours.' He rifled in his wallet and tossed down a twenty. 'Make it worthwhile.'

When Kaley added another ten to the pile it flitted through her brain that if her sister found out about this she'd kill her.

'You've got until Wednesday morning.'

'It's a deal. You hold on to the money.' He shooed her away. 'I've got work to do. Go annoy someone else. Why don't you start with our red-haired chef?'

Kaley spotted Jacca fiddling with the coffee machine and rushed across to stop him.

'What do you think you're doing?'

'Careful.' He pushed her hand away. 'Don't burn us both because you're mad.'

'Who says I'm mad?'

'If you were a kettle you'd have steam coming out of your head. I saw you were getting busy.' He lowered his voice. 'Give me a break.'

'Why should I?'

'Have dinner with me tonight and I'll explain. At least I'll try.'

'I can't.'

'I'll grovel, Kaley. Anything you want.'

'I'm not being awkward. Promise.' She managed a smile. 'Our folks haven't seen Connie yet so we're doing the family meal thing. I'm sorry. How about Thursday?'

'That works for me.' He glanced at the scones on the counter.

'Next time pull the lavender and lemon curd from the oven two minutes earlier. The edges are getting hard and if you don't sell them today they'll need to be tossed. That wastes money you don't have.' Jacca gave her a quizzical look. 'Sorry, I thought you could handle constructive criticism.'

'I can.'

'But not from me?'

If she agreed it would sound childish but Kaley couldn't lie so she said nothing.

'Your sister's a chatterbox.'

'Dare I ask what she told you?'

'If you're good at dinner tomorrow I might tell you.'

'I'm always good. Enjoy your scones.' Kaley fled to the safety of the kitchen and fanned herself with a magazine to cool her burning face.

'Have you finished slobbering over my sister?' Connie teased him as he set their coffee and scones tray down on the table.

'I wasn't slobbering.' He joined her and took a quick swig of coffee. 'Look I know we've only just met but one word of advice, don't rush into signing anything with Cash Harrison.'

'What's it to do with you? Kaley had no right to tell you about our dad.'

'Your father?' Jacca was puzzled. 'What's he got to do with you selling this place?'

'It's private.'

'Perhaps I could help.'

'You?' she scoffed. 'Do you happen to have half a million dollars lying around looking for a good home?' The colour drained from her face when he didn't immediately respond.

'What's wrong?' Kaley rushed over and stared between the two of them.

'Nothing. We're swapping stories about baking disasters that's all.'

'Yeah, right. If that's true why does she look as though Dracula rose from the grave and you've got your guilty red-faced thing going on again?'

'Let's talk somewhere quiet.' Jacca jumped up and ignored Connie's fierce glare. He steered Kaley back into the kitchen. He quietly ran through his conversation with Connie.

'I wasn't being nosy and she didn't give me any details but I get the impression you need a significant amount of money to help your father?' This wasn't the right moment to mention Cash. 'I wish you told me.'

'Why? So I could take advantage of you because you're rich?'

'Do you think that little of me . . . and yourself?'

'No, but we haven't known each other long enough to share personal stuff.'

The shop doorbell tinkled and he sighed. 'Tomorrow night I'll pick you up at six if that's OK and we'll sort this out properly.'

Shock Revelation

'You've got to give the doctor an answer this Friday?' Kaley's stomach churned.

'We don't expect you girls to perform a miracle.' Her mother's voice cracked. 'We've got an appointment with the bank tomorrow afternoon about extending our overdraft.'

They all knew that the chance of the bank coming through was minuscule at best and hopeless at worst.

'We've got a couple of ideas but I don't know if any of them will come off.' That was an exaggeration but surely a little hope was better than none?

'Promise me you won't start begging on the streets.' Her father's gentle humour made her ache for life's inherent unfairness. Knowing that the possibility of easing his chronic pain could be derailed by a simple lack of money ripped her apart.

'Drat. I didn't expect you to guess our strategy that fast.'

'I've always seen right through you, honey.' His quiet words struck home.

'We ought to go.' Kaley hugged her father, keen to end the difficult conversation.

Outside her sister wriggled into the front passenger seat of the Prius she'd rented to have something to get around in.

'Hopefully I'll be off those stupid crutches next week.' Connie huffed. 'Are you and Jacca back on track?'

'I'm not sure but we're having dinner tomorrow night.'

'I won't say another word.' Connie theatrically zipped her mouth shut.

The unaccustomed silence might last for five minutes, if she was lucky. Jet-lag stepped in to rescue her and by the time they reached the bakery her sister was happy to disappear up to the flat and leave Kaley to get back to work.

The door knob rattled and she spotted a familiar face peering through the glass.

'What do you want? It's not tomorrow yet.'

'You.'

'Very subtle.' She grabbed her keys and unlocked the door.

'I arrive bearing gifts.' A tempting aroma oozed out of the white boxes in his arms. 'Are you going to talk to me?' Jacca grinned. 'Of course, staring in admiration works, too. I'm not complaining.'

'You are so vain.'

'Hey, you're the one standing with your mouth gaping open.' His warm finger landed on her top lip.

'Your baking smells incredibly tempting. Satisfied?'

Jacca set the boxes down and opened one of the lids.

She gave in and seized one of the butterscotch bars. Kaley sunk her teeth in and the rush of sweet yumminess soothed her overwrought mind.

'Oh, Jacca.' A sob caught in her throat.

'Tell me what's wrong.' He wrapped his arms around her and she couldn't help burrowing her head against his firm, warm chest for a few magical moments.

'It's my father.' Kaley explained the

full story. 'The doctor gave him a dead-line of Friday to decide about starting the new drug.'

She eased away from him and smoothed her hands over her jeans, stained with flour and grease after a hard day in the kitchen.

'And before you offer I'm not taking your money.'

'Why not? I can't believe you would put pride before your father's health.'

'He'd agree with me a hundred per-cent.' Kaley struggled to sound more certain than she felt.

'I might have a viable alternative.' Jacca chose his words carefully. 'I'm going to a meeting late tomorrow evening which might help to solve your problem.'

Sandy had set up a meeting with Nico Chastain for tomorrow evening and he put his foot down when Jacca com-plained that he already had plans.

'Change them. It took a lot of hard work to get him interested. Nico wants us to come to the restaurant around eleven o'clock after he finishes dinner service.'

'How?' Kaley's words brought Jacca back to the present.

'I can't say yet.' He met her dark, worried gaze. 'Trust me. Please.'

'I want to.'

'Fair enough. Are you up for eating an early dinner tomorrow?'

'That's fine.' Kaley exhaled another sigh. 'There's something else. It's not serious on the level of my dad and all that but I've interfered in something I shouldn't have done.' She poured out a convoluted story about her matchmaking attempt between Connie and John Green. 'He fancied her but didn't have the nerve to make the first move until I . . . '

'Stirred him up?'

Her cheeks burned.

'I was only trying to help. What am I going to do?'

'Be honest and tell her the truth?'

'That's a terrible idea. Trust me. I guess I just needed to admit how dumb I'd been to someone.' She pointed to the cake box.

'I ought to check on Connie. Do you

113

want to come with me and bring those along?'

'Of course.' Jacca picked up the box and followed her up the narrow stairs.

'I won't ask why he's here.' Connie yawned at them from the sofa.

'I brought cake but I'll go away if you prefer.' His offer made Kaley grab the other end of the box.

'Remove those butterscotch bars from this room and I'll never speak to you again.'

'Let me think about that a minute.'

'You two are weird.' Connie looked despairingly at them both. 'I don't have a clue what's in that box but let's see if they're worth fighting over.'

Kaley opened the lid and wafted the box under her sister's nose.

'Eat that and weep.'

Jacca smiled when Connie polished one off in a couple of large bites and quickly selected another.

'Wow, that's amazing. I'm taking this one to bed with me. I'll leave you two to . . . whatever.'

Kaley's face lit up.

'I'll carry the cake. You can hop on your crutches.'

'If you aren't careful I'll change my mind and stay here until he gives in and goes home.'

'It's OK.' He touched Kaley's arm. 'You've got an early start in the morning. I need to go anyway.' When her smiling eyes were on him, Jacca knew he'd do anything to keep her looking at him that way.

* * *

Jacca strolled into the hotel lobby and startled when someone called out his name.

'Please don't rush off. I'd like a quick word.' Helen Black was loitering by one of the fake potted plants. 'Is Mr Vitale with you?'

'He's out on a date.' A complete lie but she wouldn't get the chance to mock his friend again if he had any say in it.

'Oh.' Two splotches of heat coloured

her cheeks. 'Maybe you can pass on what I came to say.'

'Maybe.'

'Could we go somewhere a little more private to talk?' Helen pointed away from the reception desk where two over-sized grey leather sofas stood in front of a stone fireplace. 'Over there?'

'I suppose.'

Neither of them made a move to sit down.

'Does Chastain know you're here?' He tried to figure out what exactly was going on.

'Yeah, but he thinks I'm making a fuss about nothing.'

'You don't?'

'No.' Helen's embarrassment deepened. 'It was juvenile of me to flirt with Sandy and lead him on and make fun of him when he made a pass at me.'

'Then why did you?'

'Bad judgement on my part. We had just won a big contract to expand into the southwest and cracked a bottle of Jack Daniels in the kitchen before we came to the charity do.'

'Putting you in the mood to play with a couple of newcomers to town?' Jacca couldn't hide his disdain.

'I'm afraid so.'

If they couldn't draw a line under the other evening the prospect of doing business together would disappear out of the window.

'Let's forget it and move on. We've all done things we aren't proud of.'

'Thank you.' Helen hesitated. 'Do you think Sandy will forgive me, too?'

'Is that important?'

'He's a good guy.' She stared down at the floor. 'I really like him. OK?' Her face lit up like a bonfire night fireworks display. 'Will you pass on what I said? I mean apart from . . . you know.'

'Don't spoil things by missing out my favourite part.' Sandy's deep laugh made Helen jump out of her skin.

Jacca had spotted his friend approaching them but purposely kept quiet.

'Where did you come from? I was watching the front door.' She turned pale. 'Oh, no! How long were you standing there?'

'I came out of the lift.' Sandy grinned. 'I was here long enough.'

'I'm off to bed . . . if anyone's interested.'

Neither of them paid Jacca any attention.

★ ★ ★

Another sleepless night equalled another ridiculously early start. Kaley slammed the scone dough on the counter and pounded it into submission. She remembered Jacca's warning about the previous batch.

'You've slightly overworked it. Remember it's not the same as making bread where you're looking to develop the gluten.'

She rolled the useless mess into a ball and aimed for the rubbish bin in the corner but blobs of raw dough splattered across her clean floor.

'Is it all right if I come in?' Cash

118

poked his head around the back door. 'Everything OK?'

'Does it look like it?' Her caustic response didn't dent his white-toothed smile. 'Why are you here?'

'To talk business.'

'At six o'clock in the morning?'

'Best time to catch a baker.'

The man had an answer for everything.

He pulled out a stool and hitched one leg up to make himself comfortable.

'Any coffee going?'

'Try Starbucks.'

'Irritable this morning, aren't we?'

She ignored him and started to scrape dough off the floor.

'Has Connie made her mind up about my proposition yet?'

'You'll have to ask her yourself. I'm not her keeper.'

'I expect she's comparing offers.' Cash's voice took on a sharp edge. 'Did you know I offered Jacca Hawken a partnership in my Dixieside development plans?'

Her shocked silence broadened his

twisted smile.

'He's been dangling me on a string and now I hear on the restaurant grapevine that he and Nico Chastain are in discussions to join forces and replace my scheme with one of their own. They'll rip this bakery to the ground in the process.'

The cleaning rag dropped out of her hand.

'I'm guessing he couldn't believe his luck when you fell in his lap.' He slid off the stool and loomed over her.

'Hawken sussed out our past history and didn't appreciate me treading on what he considers his territory. He thinks this will stop me trying to win you back.'

Kaley's brain whirred like a hamster on a plastic wheel.

'Jacca told me you ordered him to stay away from me because you had some crazy idea of us getting back together. I don't believe any of this other nonsense.'

'That's your choice.' Cash brushed away a fleck of white flour dust from his immaculate black jacket. 'You might tell Connie to think carefully before she makes her decision.'

'Is that a threat?'

'Threat?' he scoffed. 'I've got the planning commission on my side.'

'I've got work to do even if you don't. I'll pass on your message to my sister.'

'You do that, sweetheart.' Cash aimed a kiss at her mouth but she shifted in the nick of time so his dry lips only brushed her cheeks.

'I've never found another woman to equal you. We'll be a great couple again — you'll see.'

'Get out please and stay out.'

'I'll be back.'

Kaley yelled out her frustration as he disappeared out the back door.

'Who got you all riled up?' Connie limped into the kitchen.

Which piece of bad news should she tell her sister first?

* * *

'Who took away my grumpy manager and replaced him with Little Miss

Sunshine?' Jacca's complaint had zero effect on Sandy who continued drinking something that resembled moss green sludge. 'I'm guessing you fell for Helen's apology?'

'Nothing is going to spoil my good mood this morning so you might as well give up.' He punched Jacca's arm.

'Feel free to gripe about your love life because for once mine's on track and looking good.' He laughingly dragged out the last word. 'Any idea where you take a chef out for dinner to impress them?'

'Why ask me? I'm still trying to arrange a dinner date with Kaley and it's looking more unlikely by the day.'

Sandy checked his watch.

'You've got five minutes to moan.'

'Why, where are you going? Aren't we free until tonight?'

'I've got an appointment with Helen's personal trainer at her gym.' His ruddy face darkened. 'Don't give me any grief. You've been nagging me for years to do something about this.' Sandy jiggled his stomach with a rueful smile.

'Good luck.'

'Don't give up on yours yet. She's worth a bit of hassle.'

'I'm going for a run.' Jacca dragged himself off the sofa. 'See you later.'

After he pounded off his frustration he planned to head back to Franklin. Before the meeting with Nico he needed to size up Cash's plan in more detail and consider what they might do differently.

The Whole Truth

Kaley sneaked a surreptitious glance at Connie and John Green who were absorbed in conversation. It took her sister by surprise when he asked her to get a cup of coffee and join him, which could be why she accepted without a murmur. All of a sudden her sister got up and hobbled over.

'I've called Mama to tell her I don't need a ride to the hospital. John has offered to take me to get the plaster off.'

'John?'

'Don't sound so amazed.'

Kaley almost asked if they were talking about the same café hermit who used to sit in the corner and not speak to anyone but that would be asking for trouble.

'We'll probably stay out for lunch, too.'

'Lunch?'

'Yeah. Strange concept, I know, but normal people often share a meal.' Connie rolled her eyes. 'I'm going upstairs to get my coat and then we'll be off.'

This was all Kaley's fault in the first place so she shouldn't resent her sister accepting John's offer. Losing 20 dollars wasn't a big deal but maybe it stuck in her throat because she was marooned here slaving away to keep the business afloat.

'I do appreciate everything you're doing and I'll get up early with you tomorrow and help out.'

'But you can't . . . '

'There are plenty of things I can do sitting down.' A smile played with the edges of Connie's mouth. 'Be honest, the truth is you don't want me interfering with your little domain. You're afraid I'll mess up your flashy new menu.'

Did everyone see right through her?

'Not at all. I . . . we need to chat later. There's something I've got to run by you.'

'Tell me now.'

'I can't.' She couldn't explode Cash's bombshell in the middle of the work day.

'Or won't. Fine. Keep your silly little secret. I bet it's all nothing anyway.'

Kaley wished that were true.

As Connie was heading towards the car, she saw Jacca ambling along Dixie Street deep in thought.

'Hey, Red, ' she called. 'If you're goin' in there put your flak jacket on.'

'That bad?'

'Worse.' She pointed to her plaster. 'I'm getting rid of this today.'

He smiled to see John Green waiting patiently with the car door open. Kaley's matchmaking scheme must be working.

'Bulletproof vest in place.' Jacca thumped his chest.

'You'll need it. Good luck.'

He had barely opened the bakery door before Kaley glanced up from rearranging the scones and pinned him with a fierce glare.

'Am I losing my mind? Did I phone you by mistake? Because if I didn't then why are you here?'

'Perhaps I came for an early lunch.'

She waved her arm around the empty café.

'There are plenty of spare seats. Help yourself.'

'Is business slow today?' That question earned him a scathing eye roll. They were the only two people in the shop.

'Yeah. Does that make you happy? I guess you win either way.'

Alarm bells jangled in his head.

'What do you mean?'

'You took me for a fool. Big mistake.' Kaley strode across the room and planted herself in front of him, hands on hips.

'Our mutual friend Cash Harrison stopped by earlier and took great pleasure in spreading the news about your involvement in his Dixieside scheme and the other one you're trying to cook up. You've certainly been busy.'

Her words slashed through him.

'Wasn't flirting with me and taking advantage of my dad's medical problems carrying things a bit far?'

Convincing Kaley that he had genuinely fallen for her with no agenda involved could be more challenging than climbing Mount Everest in a snowstorm.

'Will you at least let me try to explain? It's not how it seems.'

'Feel free.' Her dismissive glance took in his empty hands. 'No butterscotch bar bribery today? You're slacking.'

'Sorry. It's simply me.' His weary sigh seemed to pull her up short for a few seconds.

'Fine.' She flopped down on the nearest chair and stuck out her long legs.

Jacca crossed his fingers and prepared to tell the truth, the whole truth and nothing but the truth.

'Why don't you start by telling me exactly what Cash said?'

Kaley stared at him in disbelief.

'Do you think I was born yesterday? You tell me everything first and we'll see if the stories match.'

'Fair enough,' Jacca conceded. 'I told the absolute truth when I said Sandy and I came here simply to raise my profile in America. I had met Cash at a competition in Vienna and if I don't say this bit Sandy is bound to blab . . . there is a possibility he cheated me out of winning.

'Nothing could be proved so I've tried to give him the benefit of the doubt. He told me to look him up if I ever made it to Nashville.'

'Which you did and that's when he let you in on his little moneymaking scheme to destroy this area.' Her bluntness made him wince.

'I'm always looking for new investment opportunities and it sounded like it might be a good fit. When Cash first told me about his plans he never mentioned ripping down the bakery — that only came in later. Sandy was never keen on us getting involved but I talked him around.'

The worry lines deepened around his mouth and eyes.

'I admit I did come to Franklin that first morning specifically to check out Dixie Street and the bakery.'

The next question almost stuck in her throat.

'Was I simply a bonus?'

'No!'

She didn't think he was a good enough actor to fake the horror on his face.

'Did you know about the connection

between me and Cash before the three of us met?'

'No. I swear I didn't.'

Against all logic she believed him.

'Harrison's still carrying a torch for you.'

'I realise that now but I didn't at the time,' she admitted. 'I have no interest in rekindling anything with Cash. I learned my lesson where he was concerned years ago.'

Kaley rubbed her hands on her jeans.

'We dated most of my senior year of college but I was starting to have doubts about him and they were confirmed a few weeks before graduation.

'I was hanging out with some friends one evening when Cash was supposedly 'studying for finals' but I spotted him at a bar wrapped around a blonde cheerleader called Mitzi.'

'You tackled him?'

Kaley couldn't help smiling.

'I did better than that. I waited until he proposed in front of our families on graduation day and told him exactly where he could go and why.'

'Wow. I bet that felt good?'

'Yeah, but it also made me cautious of trusting my own judgement.' Jacca's cheeks lit up and she knew her warning had hit home. 'Let's get back to talking about the bakery. What's all this about a second plan?'

'Sandy floated the idea of coming up with something far more beneficial to the area and with different investors. We're meeting Nico Chastain tonight to sound him out. I've no idea if it'll go anywhere but . . . ' She caught his quick intake of breath. 'I'm definitely not going in with Harrison. That's non-negotiable.'

Kaley frowned.

'I'm afraid Connie's on the verge of accepting his offer and I suspect others around here will, too, because everyone's struggling.'

'I really hope they don't rush into it. I see a real possibility of boosting the area if it's done the right way.' Jacca grasped her hand.

'Let me put up the money for your

father's treatment. Please. Consider it a loan. If Connie is tired of running the bakery, that's one thing, but if she's ready to fight for its survival this will balance the odds.'

'If we accepted your money, and it's a huge if, what are your ideas for Dixie Street?'

'At the moment they're fluid.' Jacca cracked a wry smile. 'Which means I don't honestly know. I should get a better idea after talking to Nico. If he's not interested then I can't pull it off alone and I'd have to look elsewhere for backing.'

'Do you think he'd be interested in a three way partnership with me?'

'You?'

She didn't blame him for sounding dumbstruck.

'Yeah. I can bring some money to the table, I'm familiar with the area and I'd love to see Franklin's new prosperity spread around more.'

'Come with us to the meeting tonight.'

'Won't Nico mind?'

'I can't see why.'

Kayley wasn't one hundred percent convinced about the wisdom of giving him a second chance but decided to go with it for now.

★ ★ ★

For once Jacca used his so-called fame and nabbed them a prized table at one of the popular new Nashville eateries. The Marsh House restaurant with its extensive seafood menu reflected his old friend John Besh's New Orleans background and the coastal influenced décor with its abundance of stainless steel, dark granite and cool greys and blues was soothing on the eyes.

'I don't need impressing.'

'Is that what I'm doing?'

'Maybe.' Kaley chewed the olive from her martini. 'You said on the way over you had a funny story to tell about Sandy?'

He'd prefer to work on the wariness lurking in her eyes but she would clam up if he tried to rush her. Jacca made her laugh by playing up his old friend's ineptness in the gym and Sandy's inherent distrust of any food that wasn't fried or smothered in ketchup.

'So where's he taking Helen for dinner?'

'She can eat at fancy places any day of the week so I suggested keeping it simple. They're at the original Martin's restaurant in Nolensville for Pat's whole hog barbecue.'

'Perfect.'

Jacca changed the subject. 'Last week Sandy asked me if making the Red Hawk brand a success here in America was still a big deal.'

'How did you reply?'

'I told him I needed to do some hard thinking.'

'And have you?' Kaley probed.

'What?'

'Thought.'

Jacca stared at her glossy red lips.

'Oh, yes. I've certainly done that.'

The Game Has Changed

Kaley's heart thudded as the noisy chatter around them appeared to fade away and Jacca's startling blue eyes sparkled under the lights. Tonight he'd crept several notches up from his usual casual attire in slim-fitting dark trousers, a blue and white striped shirt and smart tan loafers instead of his trademark red plastic clogs. His striking hair brushed his broad shoulders and when they'd walked into the restaurant she wasn't the only woman throwing admiring glances his way.

'First I need you to understand why I thought making it here was a big deal.'

She felt for him as a sad, halting story emerged of a boy desperate for validation in his mother's eyes.

'I've always been competitive. Nature or nurture — who knows? When I fell in love with baking I set out to reach the top and in many ways I've achieved my goal.'

'And now?'

'The game has changed. I need a life outside the kitchen.'

'I can't see you giving up baking.' Kaley couldn't resist challenging him. 'It's in your blood the same as computers are in mine.'

'But does it have to be all-consuming?' Jacca's smile verged on melancholy. 'Don't you want something more? Am I on the wrong track in thinking you've had enough of California? I thought we might be on the same page. Have you any idea how much I've come to . . . care for you?'

'Maybe. And maybe I feel the same way about all of those things, including you, but I can't be sure. I'm about as far out of my comfort zone here as I've ever been.' Kaley couldn't decide if it was good or bad timing when their waiter reappeared.

'Here you go, guys. Momma's gumbo for you, ma'am, and the Porter Road dirty rice and southern vegetable kimchi for you, sir.'

Her appetite had disappeared but Jacca scooped up a forkful of the steaming hot pork and rice mixture and popped it in his mouth.

'This is good. I'm glad we passed on ordering appetisers to save room for dessert.'

'Because?'

'It's the best part of the meal.'

'Forget about that for a minute.' She couldn't resist playing devil's advocate. 'Let's talk simply about the work side of things for a moment. What happens if you change your mind or the Franklin redevelopment plan falls through?'

Jacca set his fork down.

'Don't get me wrong, I'd enjoy working on it but there are plenty of other options. Sandy wants me to market the butterscotch bars commercially.' His embarrassment was endearing.

'But how I feel about you . . . that gets deeper every day.' He glanced over at the noisy after-work crowd gathered around the bar.

'Would you mind if we left? I'm not a

fan of pouring my heart out within hearing of a bunch of rowdy kids.'

'And skip dessert? Won't the sky fall in?'

'No, but I might fall apart if I don't get you to myself in the next few minutes.'

'Oh.' The blunt declaration pulled the rug out from under her feet.

'I'll take care of the bill then we'll get out of here and walk.'

'But it's cold and probably going to rain.'

'For heaven's sake — I've got an umbrella, a thick coat and warm arms to wrap around you. How many more roadblocks can you throw in our way?' Jacca sounded exasperated.

A curl of panic unravelled inside her. Ever since she broke up with Cash she had concentrated on her work and avoided any serious relationships.

Now this fascinating, mercurial man had wriggled under her skin when she wasn't looking and was getting perilously close to her heart.

'Oh, I can't handle this. Why did you

have to spoil everything?' She jerked her chair back and pushed her way out of the restaurant, almost bumping into a couple of customers.

Somehow she made her way back to Franklin and rushed up to Connie's apartment. Kaley found her sister and John cuddled up on the sofa together and as soon as they paused the film they were watching she poured out the story of her disastrous evening.

'You did what?' Connie shrieked. 'You told the poor guy he was spoiling things and walked out on him when he was trying to say he loves you? How could you?'

So much for sisterly sympathy.

'Maybe he took her by surprise.' John's tentative suggestion touched her. 'She might wish she'd reacted differently now?'

'I'm not sure.' She would never forget Jacca's stricken expression when she cut him dead.

'Why don't you sit down?' John's kindness almost undid her and she bit back tears.

139

'Jacca always reckons that baking helps him sort things out in his head so I'm gonna give it a try.'

'Stay here with us.' Connie urged.

'Leave her be, honey. She knows what she needs better than we do.'

Kaley hoped her sister realised that John was a smart man and would treat him better than her previous boyfriends.

'I'll see you later.'

When she set foot in the bakery she experienced the same calmness as when she set out to tackle a challenging computer programme. Kaley gathered her ingredients together and got busy but in a small corner of her brain she fully expected Jacca to turn up.

As the clock ticked towards 10 o'clock her confidence ebbed away and the sight of the wire racks loaded with fragrant scones, muffins and cookies did nothing to eradicate the heavy weariness engulfing her.

Too tired to cry she methodically cleaned the kitchen and checked the doors were locked before turning out the lights. She had no-one to blame for the disastrous evening but herself.

* * *

'I didn't plan it, did I?' Jacca wished he could crawl under the bedcovers and stay there. 'It seemed like a smart idea at the time.'

Kaley's dazzling smile. Her challenging questions. The way she rocked that short, black lace dress. Everything had combined to addle his brain.

'Are you still up for meeting Nico?' Sandy looked dubious.

'What's the point?'

'As far as I know the world's still turning and we've still got a living to make. We might as well go and see what happens.'

'Fine.' Jacca didn't have the energy to argue.

'Unless you'd rather track Kaley down to sort things out. Perhaps you took her by surprise and she's kicking herself now?'

'Hey, she knows where I am. She can come find me.' He dragged himself off the bed. 'Give me ten minutes.' Time to slap his Red Hawk persona back on and go to work.

Half an hour later he was sitting in Sapphire, Nico's flagship restaurant, and wondering if his powers of persuasion had completely deserted him. Kaley wasn't the only one who wanted nothing to do with him.

'I'm a businessman, not a community activist.' Nico was frowning at the plans spread out on the table.

'Can't you be both?' Jacca suggested. 'It will still make money for us. You're renowned for your charity fundraising dinners and the vigorous support you give to local businesses.'

'That's a completely different kettle of fish. You're talking about renovating a whole street of shops and houses around a restaurant small enough to fit inside this bar?' Nico scoffed.

Sandy gestured towards the map.

'If Harrison's plan goes through he'll

raze Dixie Street to the ground. People's businesses, homes and livelihoods. All gone.' The older chef's expression changed from sceptical to curious. 'That's the main reason Jacca doesn't want to be a part of it.'

'He's right.' Jacca stepped in to help out. 'Plus the more I'm around Cash the less I want to work with the man.'

They all turned when the restaurant door opened and his heart flipped when Kaley strolled in.

'Sorry I'm late. I guess y'all started without me?'

'Were we expecting you?' Nico sounded bewildered. Sandy rushed to explain. 'OK, cool.' Nico nodded. 'How about a drink?' He gestured towards the bar.

'I could murder a glass of Chardonnay.'

'Always happy to oblige a beautiful girl.'

Ouch bad choice of words, mate.

'Mr Chastain. I haven't been a 'girl' for a very long time.' Kaley leaned across the bar. 'I worked hard for my PhD in computer programming and could insist on being addressed as Doctor Robertson . . . but I won't.' She took a sip of wine and set the glass back down.

'Now is anyone going to tell me more about these plans?'

After listening to the proposals, Kaley frowned.

'My main concern is that this could take several years to put together and by then the Butterscotch Bakery and the other Dixie Street businesses will have gone under. If Cash waves enough money under their noses they'll probably sell up and move on.'

'I've got a lot of experience in building a brand and that's what we're talking about here,' Jacca explained. 'It's a question of turning Dixie Street into a sought-after destination. We need to play up the 'we're off the beaten track and better for it' aspect.'

'That's what developers did a decade ago in East Nashville and that area's exploded.' Nico joined the conversation.

'Nobody wanted to live or work there but now it's the hot place.'

'I guess we could try.'

'Give me a month.' Jacca pleaded.

'OK.'

Grudging acceptance was better than nothing.

'I've got a few contacts in the Franklin local government.' Kaley's tentative suggestion was one step up from declaring the idea a complete non-starter. 'I'll sound them out.'

'My architect created the cohesive vision for my restaurants and I'll set him to work on formulating a concept for the redevelopment,' Nico suggested.

'Right.' Kaley gathered up the notes she'd been scribbling on a yellow legal pad ever since she arrived. 'It's all right for you guys but some of us have to open up again in another six hours.'

'I could wait with you until your taxi arrives if you like?' Jacca's question popped out and she gave him a faint shrug as though it didn't make any difference to her what he did or didn't do.

Why didn't she make things easier on herself and turn down his offer to wait with her? Her parents would say that Kaley never did 'easy'.

'Taxi for Kelly Robertson?' They stared at the grey-haired man leaning out of his car window. 'You did call for a ride?'

'Yeah, I did,' Kaley stammered, 'but . . .'

'She's changed her mind.' Jacca answered for her. 'Haven't you?'

'Have you, ma'am?'

'I guess so.' Avoiding the tough conversation wasn't going to get them anywhere.

'I don't know what game you pair are up to but I lose money when people bail on me.'

Jacca fumbled in his pocket and shoved a 20 dollar bill at the driver.

'There you go. Sorry.'

'Thanks, buddy. Feel free to call again any time.'

An awkward silence wrapped around them when they were left alone.

'Just tell me where I stand.'

'About a foot away.' In her mind she added: and looking at me that way again so I can't think straight.

'I see the problems as clearly as you do.'

'Really?'

His bright blue eyes bored into her.

'But I see them as something to tackle together and I'm not sure you've reached that point yet. Am I right?'

Kaley sucked in a couple of deep, steadying breaths.

'I'm afraid.'

'And you think I'm not? I made a plan years ago for how I wanted my future to evolve, but things happen or people come into your life you don't expect and everything changes.' He gave a brief shrug. 'One of the reasons I'm successful in business is my ability to go with the flow and adapt.' Jacca looked sheepish. 'But doing the same in my personal life? I'm not so hot on that score.'

'Me neither.'

'Let's concentrate on the simpler part

first. Would it be convenient for me to come over and meet your parents tomorrow? We can broach the loan idea with them.' He cleared his throat. 'We'll leave the rest on the back burner for now.'

'You can't stay away from the food analogies, can you?'

'You would use computer ones if I understood them.'

'True. You can't help being a technophobe.'

'At least my mother didn't have to show me how to turn on an oven.' Jacca's smile disappeared and she watched his mind go to a darker place.

'Do my birth parents define who I am now?'

'No.'

'So your father cleared off and your mom won't win the Mother of the Year award any time soon,' Kaley challenged him. 'Live with it like the rest of us.'

'You're right.' He stroked her cheek. 'It's late. You'll be exhausted in the morning.'

'I'll order another taxi.' She pulled out

her phone and made a quick call.

'Do you need my help at the bakery tomorrow?'

'Connie's more mobile now so we should be good. Why don't you turn up around five in the afternoon and we'll go together over to my folks' house?'

'Do they know about me?'

He sounded like a nervous teenager.

'Some. But it could be awkward.'

'Worthwhile things often are.'

'Oh gee, it's you pair again.' The same driver grimaced out at them as he pulled up to the kerb. 'You want to cut to the chase and give me the cash now so I can go home to bed?'

'She's actually going this time. Sorry, mate.'

Far too soon Kaley found herself settled into the back of the car while Jacca passed the man a wad of cash and gave her a cheerful wink.

It would take a lot of thinking tonight to work out what just happened between them.

Wicked Attack

Jacca straightened his shoulders and met Spencer Robertson's uncompromising stare. It wasn't ideal to meet a man for the first time and offer him a bundle of money.

'You mean well, son, but I don't know you from Adam. I'm sure you're a decent enough guy and you obviously care for my little girl but there's no way I'm taking your money.'

'I've forgiven you a lot of things in my time, Spencer Robertson, but this ain't gonna be one of them.' Lorna glared at her husband. 'Your gravestone will say 'He wouldn't be here now if he listened to his wife'.'

'Don't you have any pride?' Spencer asked.

'Let me have a good ole think about that.' She pretended to look thoughtful. 'Dead husband or pride. Which would I prefer?'

'There's no guarantee the treatment

will work.' Spencer's voice softened.

'But if you don't try you'll never know,' Lorna begged. 'You've never quit on me before.'

'I'm not quitting.'

'Yes, you are.' She pointed to Connie and Kaley. 'And on them. Aren't you gonna fight for the chance to see them married and be here for your grandchildren?'

'That's underhand. I'm sorry, honey, but this is . . . hard for me.' Beads of sweat stood out on his pale forehead.

'I totally understand, sir.' Jacca jumped in again. 'I heard once that a mark of maturity is being able to accept help.'

'It sure is, Daddy.' The colour rose in Kaley's face and she couldn't quite meet his gaze. They both knew that they were hopeless examples of that themselves.

'I've heard enough.' Connie jabbed a pointy finger at her father. 'If you don't accept Jacca's generous offer right now I'll never speak to you again. Tomorrow morning you tell that doctor to go ahead with the treatment.'

'OK, OK.' Spencer flung his arms in the air. 'Stop hassling me, all of you. I'll do it.' He raised an eyebrow in Jacca's direction. 'If the offer's still open?'

'Of course.'

'But only as a loan and it will be paid back, I just don't know when.'

'Fair enough. No conditions.' Jacca needed Kaley to realise he wasn't exerting any pressure on her.

Connie grinned.

'I reckon a coffee would go down well right now.'

'We'll have homemade pecan pie to go with it,' Lorna declared. 'Go and fix it, Kaley.'

'Me? Slogging away in the bakery all day isn't enough?'

'I'll help.' Jacca aimed her towards the kitchen.

'I'll see to the coffee while you cut five slices.' Kaley pointed to a golden brown pie sitting on the counter.

'By the way,' Jacca said, 'Sandy's rescheduled our upcoming UK plans and confirmed our slot at the Nashville food and drink festival in September.

'He's also hired a local PR person to help with promoting the whole of Dixie Street and we've got several media interviews set up for next week.'

'Already?' Kaley sounded amazed. 'Wow! You don't waste time.'

'Life's too short.' He peered over her shoulder. 'We ought to get cracking — we don't want your mother in here checking on us.'

'Yeah, yeah. Stop nagging.'

'Fix an extra slice of pie.' Connie bustled in. 'John just arrived.'

'Why?'

'Because I invited him. Is that a problem?'

'No, of course not.'

Kaley's forehead wrinkled in a deep frown as her sister left.

'If she ever finds out about the bet I'm toast, and John will be, too.'

'You could be honest and tell her. Things are working out well between them so she might not mind too much.'

'Trust me. I know Connie better than

you.' She shook her head.

Jacca got the extra plate ready and stacked all six up his arms, waiter style. Before he could open the door Connie strode back in.

'Here, you can help.' Kaley held out a couple of mugs to her sister. 'Take these out to Mom and Dad.'

'They can wait.'

'What's wrong?' Connie's grim expression registered with him.

'Why don't you tell me? What's all this about a bet?'

The temperature in the room plummeted.

Kaley's stomach twisted in a painful knot.

'Don't pussyfoot around — I was listening at the door.'

This wouldn't end well.

'Shall I go out there and ask John instead?'

'No.' The last thing they needed was a full scale row in front of their parents. 'You had a lousy time in Switzerland with your broken leg and that loser Simon bailing on you. I found out John fancied you . . .'

'And thought you'd interfere.' Connie's face tightened.

'John wanted to ask you out but didn't have the nerve. I prodded him, that's all.'

'How much was I worth?'

'Don't put it that way.' It sounded terrible spelled out so bluntly.

'How would you like me to put it?'

'What on earth's going on?' Lorna burst in and glared around at them all. 'Your daddy's getting agitated with all this yelling and that's not good for him.'

'You tell her,' Connie snapped.

She caught Jacca's resigned shrug and knew she had no alternative. Kaley raced through the story and waited for the condemnation to start.

'That wasn't the smartest idea you've ever had but your heart was in the right place, sweetheart.' Her mother sighed.

'So that makes it all right?' Connie's voice rose to a shrill screech. 'I don't think so.' She stormed out of the kitchen. 'John Green, you're a conniving loser.

Get out of this house right now.'

'Wait a little while, please. Your father suggested we talk this through in the dining-room. In private.'

Kaley couldn't decide if John was courageous or simply oblivious to the fury pouring off her sister.

'I'm not going anywhere with you ever again!' Connie yelled.

'We can sort this out, sweetheart.' He grasped her sister's arm and steered her out of the room.

'Should we . . . '

'Leave them alone.' Her father cut Kaley off before she could finish.

Jacca squeezed her shoulder.

'Let's be on our way.' He turned back to Spencer. 'Let us know what the doctor says and we'll sort out the loan details from there.'

Her father's eyes glazed over.

'I don't know how to thank you.'

'Then don't try. I'm happy to step in. End of story.'

'But you haven't eaten your pie.' Her mother's protest made Kaley smile. She was as bad as Jacca when it came to feeding people. 'Take it with you.' Lorna disappeared back to the kitchen and returned with two foil covered plates. 'Off you go.' She handed over the desserts then smacked a loud kiss on Jacca's cheek. 'That's from both of us.'

Before her family could completely smother him, Kaley whisked him away.

⋆ ⋆ ⋆

Kaley snuggled into Jacca on Connie's sofa.

'I keep forgetting to ask but how is Sandy's romance coming along?' she said.

'OK I think, although the jury is still out on whether Helen Black will turn him into a health nut or kill him. She dragged him out for a run around Radnor Lake late this afternoon and then they were going to eat dinner together.' Jacca chuckled.

'I'm fairly certain he didn't tell her that the last time he ran was at a primary school sports day back in the Dark Ages.'

She gave him a searching look.

'He's family to you, isn't he?'

It was an effort to smile and nod.

'Do you have any contact with your mother?'

'Yes, but not a lot. Where does all this come from, anyway? It's not just Sandy, is it?' Jacca knew he was avoiding the question.

'I guess seeing my unique family dynamic tonight got me thinking,' Kaley explained. 'In case you were wondering but didn't like to ask my birth mother passed away before my first birthday and I've never had any desire to track down my biological father.

'He knew I existed but never came back to Jamaica, offered her any help or ever tried to contact me later on. That tells me all I need to know about him. My real father adores me and that's all I need.' Her voice wobbled. 'I don't know how I'll cope if anything happens to him.'

'You'll always carry his love for you here.' Jacca pressed her hand against her racing heart.

'I know.' A shadow settled on her beautiful face. 'What about your father?' 'I've no clue and I don't care.' 'Really?' Heavens, she knew him better than anyone. It didn't make sense after a few short weeks but some things simply were.

'No, not really.' He dropped his head. 'I've never admitted that to Sandy and I tell him most everything.'

'You could trace him.'

'What's the point?'

'Maybe he'll tell you why he left.'

Jacca scoffed.

'I already know.'

'If your mother was honest with you.'

'OK — maybe I'll have a stab at tracking him down.' He probably sounded grudging but she didn't call him out on it.

'Good.' Kaley's phone jangled into her Star Wars ringtone. 'What's up, Connie?' The frown deepened between her eyes. 'I'll be there soon as I can.' She hung up.

'Is your father ill?'

'No. Connie got a call to say the bakery is on fire.'

'The bakery? But you haven't done any baking for hours.'

'It could be the wiring. It's old,' Kaley suggested.

A nasty suspicion sneaked into his head.

★ ★ ★

Jacca made a beeline for the man as soon as the stranger finished talking to the policeman. He quickly introduced himself as a close friend of the Robertson sisters.

'Did you see what happened?'

'Yes, and it was quite a shock, I can tell you. That's my place.' He pointed to a large, blue house about three doors away from the bakery.

'I'm Thaddeus Brown. I was taking my dog out for the last time before we turned in for the night and I saw a man messing around with something at the front of the bakery. Next thing I know he runs off and a burst of flames shot up into the sky. It must've been some sort of incendiary device.' He shoved a hand through his short grey hair. 'I reported it right away.'

'Did they catch him?'

'Yes.' Thaddeus cracked a smile. 'He tripped on one of the loose paving stones and hurt his ankle. They've got him in custody.'

'Out of interest have you heard of a Nashville chef called Cash Harrison?'

'Oh, have I ever! The man's a complete pest. He phones me constantly and keeps coming around here and banging on my door, pestering me to sell my house.

'I told him I'll make up my mind when I'm good and ready and not before. He's been annoying all of my neighbours too.'

Jacca grasped the opportunity to explain Harrison's original Dixieside plan before comparing it to their own possible scheme.

'Something needs to be done.' Thaddeus glanced along the street and shook his head.

The end of Dixie Street closest to the

town wasn't too bad but past the bakery it deteriorated further until it ended at a derelict, empty lot by the Harpeth River.

'When I moved here forty years ago this was a thriving area. Franklin lost a lot of its old buildings before the historic preservation people stepped in to halt the decline in the centre of town back in the nineteen eighties. Unfortunately we're out on a limb here.'

A long-term resident who wasn't afraid of well thought out change would make a perfect ally.

'Would you mind if I stopped by your house tomorrow for a proper chat?'

'Not at all. Come anytime you like, I'm usually around. I'd better go now, Rusty's getting restless.' Thaddeus patted his dog's head and the massive Irish wolfhound tugged on his leash.

Jacca let him go and spotted the two sisters standing in front of the bakery with their arms wrapped around each other. As he approached, Kaley broke away to run her hand over the smoke stained paint and wiped a tear from her cheek.

'I've been chatting to Thaddeus Brown who lives in that blue house.' He gestured towards it.

'And?'

He repeated the whole conversation.

'You aren't implying Cash had anything to do with this?' Kaley sounded bewildered.

'I'm only saying it's a possibility. We can't count it out.'

'Well, I can. Cash is a lot of things but he's not an arsonist,' Kaley said firmly.

'I expect you're right. We'll wait and see what the police turn up.'

'Someone knows when to back off.' Connie chimed into the conversation. 'Not only handsome but smart, too.'

'Your boyfriend better not hear you say that.'

'It's too late.' John hurried over to join them and wrapped his arms around Connie. 'Are you OK, babe?'

'Better now you're here.'

Jacca swapped smiles with Kaley behind the other couple's backs.

John's mouth turned up at the edges.

'I may be strictly average when it comes to good looks but it doesn't seem to bother this beautiful lady.'

'That is so not true,' Connie protested.

'You're a doll to say so.'

Kaley couldn't hardly believe what she was seeing and hearing. Her sister usually dated drop-dead gorgeous men whose brainpower came in a distant second.

'That doesn't mean you are totally forgiven for interfering.' Connie glared at Kaley for a full two seconds before breaking into a broad smile. 'Let's see what it's going to take to clean up this mess.'

'The door is a write off to start with.' Jacca pulled away a charred splinter of wood. The fireman had left a gaping hole after they took an axe to it. 'We'll get a new one hung first thing in the morning. I'm happy to bed down here for the night to keep an eye on the building.'

'Is that necessary?' Kaley asked.

'You could have a problem with looters if we simply board it up and leave.'

They all followed him in and for several minutes no-one spoke. She guessed their minds were running along the same tracks. The wet, mud-streaked floor and general mess was going to be a challenge but if Thaddeus Brown's dog hadn't needed a walk at the right time things could have been ten times worse.

'I'll stay with Jacca,' John offered.

'It's my shop.' Connie shook her head. 'I should stay.'

'Your leg is still healing, sweetheart. You need to be in your proper bed.'

'I suppose you're right, thanks.'

Kaley hadn't expected her sister's swift concession.

'Why don't we dig in and start the clean-up?' Jacca suggested. 'When we've all had enough you can bring us down some pillows and blankets before you go to bed.'

'But you'll both be exhausted you won't get any sleep.'

'Doesn't matter. We can sneak in a morning nap while you and Connie do the baking.'

'Do you seriously think we'll be able to open?' She couldn't see the possibility herself.

'I don't see why not.'

Kaley didn't check to see if he had his fingers crossed behind his back.

They divided up the tasks and once they were on their own in the kitchen, something she suspected he'd engineered, Jacca wrapped his arms around her. Out of the blue the seriousness of the whole situation sunk in.

'Whoever did this could've killed Connie.' She bit back a sob.

'Or you.' His eyes darkened. 'If I get my hands on them . . . '

'I know.'

'You're everything to me.' The heart-stopping words blurted out of him and she sensed him panic.

'You can prove it by scrubbing the floor.' Please play along. When Jacca turned his easy smile back on she relaxed. For now.

Good News

Kaley wandered across to stare out of the window at the blustery, spitting rain whipping away the few remaining leaves clinging to the trees. The distance between Franklin and sunny California widened into a yawning gulf. She didn't find the idea of dealing with the everyday internal politics of the software business again the least bit tempting. With her credentials she could go freelance and pick projects that interested her and work on them from . . . here? She couldn't believe she was seriously contemplating such a radical change.

'What's going on in your pretty head now? I hear the wheels cranking.' Jacca wandered in from the kitchen carrying two mugs of tea.

Connie had shooed them out of the bakery and ordered them to go back upstairs to the flat after the early morning rush.

'I'm thinking about what you said.'

167

'You want to be more specific? I talk a lot.'

His warm smile helped to ease her doubts and Kaley tentatively explained.

'If I went down that road I'd have time to be involved in the renovation project, too, assuming it pans out.'

'And us?' The tips of Jacca's ears turned bright red.

Before she could reply her phone buzzed.

'Sorry. It's my dad.'

'Hi, baby girl. Good news. I saw the specialist this morning and he's been in touch with the drug company. They've got me into a new trial which means I get the treatment for free.'

'That's awesome!'

'Would you mind telling Jacca I sure did appreciate his offer to bail me out but I won't need to bother him now?'

'Will do. Tell Mom we'll pick up some of your favourite barbecue and bring it over for dinner. It'll save her cooking. Bye.' She repeated the update to Jacca and watched conflicting emotions flicker over his face.

'That's great. Not that I wasn't happy to lend him the money but I know he feels better this way.' His voice turned raspy. 'I wasn't conscious of trying to buy his approval but maybe I was? I should've learned my lesson. Didn't work with my mother, did it?'

'You're too hard on yourself.'

He gave a grim chuckle.

'Don't you dare say, 'Bless your heart'. I've already picked up that's the southern way of calling someone a loser.'

Kaley didn't get a chance to protest before her phone buzzed again.

'Now it's the police. We're never going to . . .'

'Answer it, we'll talk later. I'm not going anywhere.'

That quiet statement meant a whole lot. She listened to the detective with a sinking heart and somehow managed to thank him.

'They interviewed the man who's in custody and it turns out he's a known criminal. He claims Cash hired him to burn down the bakery.'

'Perhaps he's lying to save his own skin?' Jacca suggested.

'They haven't tracked down Cash yet to hear his side of the story.'

'Innocent until proven guilty, right?'

Kaley shrugged. She wasn't blind to Cash's faults but couldn't wrap her head around the fact he might have tried to harm her and Connie for the sake of a business opportunity.

'I ought to get back to work.' She sighed. 'John must be dead on his feet by now. I'm sure neither of you got a wink of sleep.'

'Concrete floors aren't the last word in comfort.' He grabbed hold of her hands and a bolt of awareness shot through her.

'After dinner tonight we're going to have some time alone if we have to find a bunker and lock ourselves in.'

★ ★ ★

'Why are men never around when you want them and under your feet every other time?' Lorna grumbled.

'What do you want Daddy for?' Kaley dumped the baked beans into a bowl and set the microwave for two minutes on high.

'It's nearly dinner time.'

'Is everything OK?' There was an edgy restlessness about her mother. 'You seem a little antsy.'

'Maybe it's because your father starts treatment on Monday and if it doesn't work . . .' Tears worked their way down Lorna's cheeks.

'You'll survive because that's what we do. I need you. Connie needs you.' Kaley's blunt statement put a stop to her mother's tears. 'Go fix your face while I pull dinner together. I'll crack the whip and round the guys up.'

'I don't know what things are comin' to when my daughter orders me around,' Lorna muttered and bustled out of the kitchen.

'Something's smelling good. How

much longer do I have to wait to try this famous barbecue?' Her dad appeared in the doorway, grinning.

Suddenly Connie burst into the kitchen with John trailing in behind her.

'Sorry we're late. I don't think the darn rain is ever gonna stop.'

'Sit yourselves down,' Lorna urged, slipping back into mother hen mode. She started to load up a massive platter with charred, smoky brisket, ribs and pulled pork. 'Dig in.' For a while the only sounds came from everyone eating and the occasional satisfied grunt.

'I made a banana pudding. Who's ready for some?'

'Oh, heavens, we're far too full, Mom.' Kaley couldn't see herself eating again before at least lunchtime tomorrow.

'Speak for yourself,' Jacca contradicted her.

'Aren't you too stuffed to think about dessert?' She laughed and smacked her head. 'Is that the stupidest thing I've ever said?'

'Pretty much.' Nobody else took up

her mother's offer and Kaley watched in a cross between awe and horror as Jacca dug in. Of course he launched a long discussion about the recipe and they debated the merits of serving banana pudding at room temperature or chilled and with or without a layer of meringue on the top. The Robertson family were all 'chilled and no meringue' people.

'Now I'm stuffed.' Jacca patted his stomach. 'I promised I'd bake a few things to help out for tomorrow so we ought to make a move.'

That would work as an excuse to leave early.

'Now you're making me feel guilty.' Connie protested. 'We've got tickets to see the new Batman movie at seven o'clock and I planned to make up for it by going in early tomorrow morning.'

'We don't mind, do we?' He glanced at Kaley for approval.

'No, of course not.'

'You're a good boy.' Lorna's praise made him blush, something that wasn't hard to achieve but more amusing than it should be. 'Off you go.'

They made their escape and collapsed in giggles outside the front door.

'Now you're stuck with doing more baking.'

'No, I'm stuck with you and that's exactly what I want. Hopefully you do, too.'

'Do you really need to ask?' His returning smile was the perfect answer.

Dramatic Turn of Events

Jacca didn't dare to initiate anything in the way of serious conversation until the kitchen was fragrant with orange coffee cakes, feta and rosemary scones and dark chocolate pecan cookies. He made two mugs of hot chocolate topped with homemade marshmallows and set them on the counter before mentally sticking a pin in the things-to-talk-about list.

'I kept my promise to you.'

'Which one?' Kaley frowned at him.

'To contact my father.' He hated to burst her bubble. 'I tracked down his e-mail address through an old friend because I couldn't face the idea of him slamming the phone down on me.' Jacca dragged a well-thumbed sheet of paper from his pocket and passed it over.

'Here's his reply. I know you wanted the fairy tale but it's not happening.' It tore him up to see her dark soulful eyes fill with emotion as she read through the letter several times.

'Oh, Jacca, I'm sorry. I shouldn't have pushed you.'

'Yes, you absolutely should.' He squeezed her hand. 'It's always niggled at me and now I can put it behind me.'

'But how could he say those things? You're his son. I hoped one of us might be lucky.'

'I am lucky.' He stroked his fingers over her thick, silky hair. 'I've got you and your family. Sandy's the best friend a man could want and the rest of the Vitale family mean an awful lot to me, too. Plus there's my mum. I'm good.'

'Yeah, I get that but it must've still hurt to read.'

Jacca gave a slight shrug. She knew the words were ingrained in his head.

'If you're after money you're barking up the wrong tree because I haven't got any. Your mum and I wouldn't have lasted anyway but having you didn't help. It's not your fault and I did you a favour by clearing off. Don't bother getting in touch again.'

'You're not your father.' Kaley spelled

out his worst fear. 'I'm a smart woman and smart women don't fall for losers.'

Underneath her smile he sensed she was exhausted.

'It's late and you need your sleep. Are you OK with us delaying the rest of our chat until tomorrow?' He rushed to reassure her. 'I'm not trying to put it off. Honest.'

'Shush. I know that.'

'I'll walk you upstairs before I go.'

'Are you afraid I might get lost or hoping for a kiss?'

'Both.' He chuckled.

'You do surprise me.'

Kaley was surprised to find the door locked and rummaged around in her handbag for her key to let them in.

'Connie must not be back yet.'

'How do you know? Everything looks . . . '

'Tidy? Exactly. That's because I was the last one out.' She wandered into the kitchen. 'My dear sister always takes a mug of coffee to bed with her but there's no sugar spilled on the counter or milk left out of the fridge.'

'Perhaps she's still out with John?'

'I'll call her.' When her sister didn't answer she left a brief message.

'Something's wrong.' A wave of relief swept through her when he didn't argue. 'I'll try Mom.' A brief conversation with Lorna ratcheted her anxiety up a few more notches. 'According to her John dropped Connie off here hours ago. I'll call him next.'

John took a while to answer and his voice was thick with sleep.

'Connie didn't say she planned to go anywhere?' The nervous knot tightened in her stomach. 'Yeah, I'll check around and get back to you.'

'I'll look around downstairs while you give the flat a thorough going over,' Jacca offered. 'Yell if you find anything.'

There weren't many places to check in the tiny flat but she searched every inch.

'Come down here, Kaley.' Jacca sounded worried.

'Where are you?' She almost tumbled down the stairs in her haste.

'Outside the back door.' He pointed at something on the ground. 'Is this Connie's?'

A red suede clutch bag lay there with its contents strewn all over the concrete. 'Yeah, it's her favourite.' Kaley swallowed hard. 'She was carrying it tonight.' She reached down to pick up a lipstick on the ground near the rubbish bins.

'Don't touch that. Leave everything where it is. We need to ring the police.'

'The police? Aren't you overreacting?'

'Do you honestly think so?'

She shook her head.

'Would you prefer me to ring them?'

'Yes, please. I'm not sure I can.'

'Come back inside.' Jacca led her back into the kitchen and somehow ended up perched on a stool with a glass of water in front of her. As he made the phone call, his voice became stronger and more insistent. Finally he ended the call.

'Someone will be here soon.'

'They don't think we're making a fuss over nothing?'

'They did at first but I put them right.'

'I should let John know. I suppose I'd better call my folks, too.'

'There's no need, your mother's already here.' He pointed towards the front door. 'I'll let her in.'

'What's going on?' Lorna frowned at them both. 'Did you find Connie?'

'Not exactly.'

'You either did or you didn't.'

Kaley ran through the whole story and saw her own fear reflected back in her mother's clear blue eyes. How would they break it to her father if something had happened to his precious daughter?

★ ★ ★

Jacca's suspicions mushroomed. It hadn't taken long for the Officer Broad to speculate about a possible connection between Connie's disappearance and the recent arson attempt on the bakery.

'So far we've been unable to contact Mr Harrison. According to his staff he left them to finish up the dinner service tonight.

'One of the waiters overheard him on the phone talking about meeting someone but there's no reason to connect it with Ms Robertson.'

'Can we do anything to help?' Kaley asked.

'You could put together a list of any friends your sister might have decided to visit or contact.'

'Have you found Connie yet?' John burst into the café and glanced wildly around at them all.

'Who are you, sir?' The policeman gave him a hard stare.

'John Green.' He stumbled over his words. 'I'm Connie's boyfriend. I dropped her as close as I could to the back entrance here around ten o'clock.'

He crumpled into the nearest chair and clasped his head in his hands.

'I wanted to park and walk in with her but she ordered me to go on home.' He managed a wan smile. 'She's not a woman you argue with.'

'We'll need a statement from you because as far as we know you're the last person who saw Ms Robertson.'

'You can't think I'd hurt her . . . I love her.' His anguish touched Jacca. 'I'll tell you anything you need but you're wasting valuable time.'

'No information is wasted when we're dealing with a missing person.' The officer put away his notebook. 'I'm going to take a look at where Ms Robertson's purse was found then I'll take you back to the police department with me, sir.'

'I'll show you.' Jacca led the way outside.

'She was probably interrupted before she could open the door.' Broad gestured to the key ring with its miniature Barbie doll charm tossed down by the steps.

'Kaley and I were working in the kitchen and we didn't see or hear anything.'

'How long have Ms Robertson and Mr Green been a couple?'

'I believe John's been a regular customer at the bakery for a couple of years but they've only been dating for a few weeks.'

182

'What do you know about Mr Green's background?'

'Not a lot but I do know he loves Connie and would never harm her,' Jacca snapped. 'I'm sorry, but we're all worried.'

'I appreciate that, sir. I'll put all this in my report and see where we need to go from there.'

All of a sudden the situation became a lot more real.

'Connie was very much alive when I left her. All right?'

Kaley couldn't bring herself to reassure John while her emotions were all over the place.

Officer Broad walked back in, followed by Jacca.

'Come along with me please, sir.'

'I hoped y'all knew me better than this.' John dragged to his feet.

'No-one's accusing you of anything. It's routine.' The policeman nodded at her mother. 'You might as well go home, ma'am. There's nothing more you can do here.'

'Home?' Lorna shrieked. 'You think I'm going to bed when my baby girl's missing?'

'Sorry, ma'am.' He backed off. 'We'll call if there's any news.'

'Thank you.' Kaley gulped down a sob.

'Hopefully it's a false alarm.'

When he ushered John out and closed the door behind them it puzzled her that Jacca didn't rush to her side.

'I better call your daddy.' Her mother sounded weary.

'Why don't you go up to the apartment and have a quiet chat?' Kaley suggested.

'All right, sweetie.'

As soon as Lorna disappeared she didn't beat around the bush with Jacca.

'What's up with you?'

'Did you try to reassure John that none of us believe he's involved in this?' She couldn't avoid his piercing stare.

'Wow, I hope if I'm ever in trouble they don't ask you for a character reference. I understand why the police have to interview him but I don't believe for

184

one second that he harmed Connie. Do you?'

'No.' Kaley felt awful.

'He needed our support.' Jacca's voice hardened. 'Not to leave here thinking we doubt him.'

Tears rolled down her face.

'I'm sorry — I didn't mean to get at you.' He rested his strong, warm hands on her shoulders. 'I understand that you're scared and your mother's scared but when I came in you and Lorna were glaring at poor John as though he was Jack the Ripper reincarnated.'

'Were we?'

A curve of amusement pulled at his top lip.

'If looks could kill he'd be a pile of bones by now.'

'You're such a good man and I love you for it.'

'I love you, too.' Jacca brushed a soft kiss on her cheek. 'We're all under a lot of strain.'

'I know there's no proof yet that Cash is involved but surely this can't be all part of some warped attempt to win me back?'

'I don't think so, honey. I suspect we're way past that. I don't know why yet but this Dixieside development seems to be crucial to him.' He frowned.

'I've thought about getting in touch with Luiz Rodriguez at the Cracked Biscuit. He might know who Harrison's close associates are, people who might be persuaded to talk to me rather than the police.'

'Anything is worth a try.' She caught his hesitation. 'Spit it out.'

'I've got an idea to help your mum but I'm not sure she'll go for it.'

Kaley read his mind in one second.

'Mom won't shift an inch from here so don't bother going down that road.'

'But what about your poor father stuck at home on his own? Worrying. What about if we promised to stay here?'

'I suppose it's worth a try.' She didn't have much faith in the plan. 'Let me take the lead. I've had years of practice handling her.'

Jacca pretended to tape his mouth shut.

'Watch the master at work.' Kaley pulled her shoulders back and marched up the stairs. Lorna was hunched over on the sofa, staring into space and looking ten years older.

'How's Daddy doing?'

'Fretting.'

'You don't think . . . no, of course not.' Kaley shook her head.

'What're you getting at?'

'I keep thinking one of us should be with Daddy before he worries himself into the hospital. Maybe I could go, or Jacca?'

'Don't be silly. It's my place.' Lorna jumped up. 'I ought to be with him. You stay here and call me the second you hear anything.' She wagged her finger at Jacca. 'You better take care of my girl here or you'll answer to me.'

'I promise I will.'

Lorna slipped on her coat and found her handbag.

'Give Daddy my love.'

When the door closed behind her mother Jacca's face cracked into a wide grin.

'You get an A-plus for that performance. She never saw it coming. I must remember you're a great actress so you don't catch me out another day.'

'We shouldn't be joking around.'

He wrapped his arms around her.

'Let's get to work.' He let go of her and pulled out his phone. 'Luiz, it's Jacca Hawken. I've got a couple of questions.'

Kaley sat at the kitchen table and opened her laptop. Over the last few years she'd pushed her family to the sidelines of her life but that's not where she wanted them to be any longer. Here was her second chance.

So Many Questions ...

Luiz struck Jacca as a plain speaking man so he didn't tiptoe around the subject.

'That's bad news, amigo.'

Jacca had half-hoped the young man would tell him not to be an idiot.

'I work here to gain experience but I won't stay a day longer than I have to. Harrison was always a tough boss but no more than most top chefs, and I can handle that. But he's become increasingly erratic recently and there are rumours he likes to gamble.'

Everything started to make sense.

'Is there anyone on the kitchen staff who might talk to me?'

'Carlos Herrara is your best bet. He's tight with the boss but if you pay him enough he might co-operate. Do you want me to call him and make up an excuse to lure him back to the restaurant?'

'If Harrison finds out he'll fire you without a decent reference.'

'I'll survive.' Luiz chuckled.

'If we get our version of this Franklin redevelopment scheme off the ground you've got a job there any time you want one.' It was the best Jacca could offer.

'Deal. I'll get on to Carlos and let you know what he says.'

Jacca paced around the room waiting for the call back and almost leapt on the phone when it rang.

'Carlos is on the way to the restaurant with some rat traps. I pretended I spotted one in the walk-in cooler when I was cleaning up and couldn't get hold of the boss to tell him.

'He thinks I'm still there but I can be there in about ten minutes from my apartment and it'll take him a good twenty or twenty-five minutes from where he lives.'

'Great. You might have to stall him but I'll be there as soon as I can.' He rang for a taxi then found Kaley in the bedroom searching through her sister's things.

'I'm off to the Cracked Biscuit. I'll call if I find anything out.'

'Be careful.'

'I will.'

The roads were quiet this late at night and they made it to Nashville in record time.

'Ah, Mr Hawken — good to see you again.' A white toothy grin lit up Luiz's swarthy features. 'Come and meet Carlos.'

A burly man with hands the size of T-bone steaks emerged from the shadows.

'What's he doing here?' His hard black eyes settled on Jacca.

Kaley discovered a pink sparkly address book adorned with mermaids and unicorns in Connie's bedside table, transcribed the details on to her laptop and sent the list off to the police, just as her phone launched into its Star Wars ringtone.

'I need you to get over to this house now.' Jacca rattled off an East Nashville address. 'Wait outside until I get there.'

'Any chance you're gonna tell me what this is about?'

'I haven't got time. Bye.'

Kaley tugged on a short red wool coat and dashed outside. The streets were deserted and once she exited the interstate at Dickerson Pike it was only a couple of blocks to find Aline Avenue.

She snagged a parking spot close enough to keep an eye on the shabby front door of number 12 and drummed her fingers on the steering wheel while she peered out into the dark night for any sign of Jacca.

A light flickered on in the house and she picked out the familiar shape of Connie's head through one of the upstairs windows.

Kaley rifled in the glove compartment for the heavy torch her father had insisted she kept there for emergencies and leapt out of the car.

She inched her way along the narrow path and crouched down behind an overgrown holly bush near the ramshackle front porch. Her phone buzzed with an incoming text message.

'Where are you? J.'

'Who's out there?' A man's deep voice

boomed into the night. 'Come out where I can see you.'

Kaley cautiously stood up and flashed her torch in his face.

'I'm Connie's sister. If you've hurt her — ' The man was twice her size and saying he didn't look very friendly was putting it mildly.

'Stand back, sweetheart.' Jacca's clipped English voice never sounded so good next to her shoulder. 'You should have listened to me, Herrara.'

'Oh yeah?' The man's sharp eyes darted around. 'Is this the cavalry come to the rescue?'

Two men appeared. One was John Green but she didn't recognise the other dark-haired man.

'Let us in. The police are on the way.'

Kaley's heart thumped when Jacca took a step forward and at the last second the man glowered and stepped to one side. She took off running past them all.

'Where do you think you're going?' Jacca yelled after her.

'To find my sister. What do you think?'

Inside there was no sign of life so she raced up the stairs.

'Connie? Where are you?'

'In a nasty, grubby bedroom. That idiot locked me in.'

Kaley sagged with relief, her knees almost buckling under her. Her sister's voice came from behind the closest door and it was a battle to steady her trembling fingers enough to turn the key in the lock.

'Are you all right?'

'Of course I'm all right but you wait until I get my hands on Cash Harrison.' Her eyes blazed.

'Did he put you here?' Kaley's head spun.

'No, but that oaf was outside the bakery waiting when I got home and spun me a line about Cash needing to talk to me about the business.' Connie shook her head. 'When I tried to get my phone out to call Harrison he knocked my bag away and forced me into his grimy old truck.'

'Did Cash ever put in an appearance?'

'Nope. That idiot kept insisting he was on the way but he never turned up.' Her sister's face lit up as she glanced over Kaley's shoulder.

John was standing on the top step with a wary look on his face.

'Come here, I need a hug.'

'Oh honey, I was so afraid for you . . . '

Kaley watched the two embrace and talk in low, intimate tones. How could she have doubted this good, kind man who loved her sister beyond anything?

Loud voices drifted up from downstairs.

'Ms Connie Robertson?' A uniformed officer rushed up. 'Can you walk downstairs or shall I get the paramedics to come up here?'

'I'm fine. I wish everyone would stop fussing.' The tender look Connie gave John belied her sharp words.

'Has anyone told our folks that she's safe?' Kaley asked.

'Not yet, ma'am,' The policeman admitted.

'I'll do it.' Connie snatched John's phone and tapped in the number.

Kaley smiled as her sister strode off downstairs with John and the policeman trailing behind her.

A shudder ran through her and she choked back tears. Luckily it had all ended well but why did it happen in the first place? That was the sixty-four thousand dollar question.

Unconditional Love

'Where on earth have you been?' Sandy wandered out of his bedroom, rubbing his bloodshot eyes. 'It's four o'clock in the morning.'

'It's a long story.' Jacca warned.

'I'll make tea. You talk.'

'Sorry I woke you.' Jacca slumped on the sofa and by the time he finished running through everything Sandy's eyes were out on stalks.

'Well, that's quite a story. I don't know about you but I'm off back to bed. You should try to snatch a few hours.'

'I'm too keyed up to sleep.' Jacca admitted. 'The girls were pretty beat when I left them and I don't see them getting the bakery open on time.'

'So Sir Galahad will ride in on his white horse to the rescue?' Sandy laughed and shook his head. 'Go on, mate.'

'Cheers.' He changed into his chef's whites, tucked the spare bakery key Kaley had given him in his pocket and headed off to Franklin. Two hours later he finished up in time to flip the sign on the bakery door to Open.

'Are you a bakery angel?' Kaley's loose ponytail was collapsing already and there were smudges of exhaustion under her eyes. To him she was still beautiful. Strong. Capable. Smart. Everything he wanted.

'How does a spinach and ham croissant warm out of the oven and a giant mug of coffee sound?' He gave her a gentle kiss and brushed a few stray curls away from her face.

'I'm afraid we've got customers waiting — not afraid because customers are a good thing but you know what I mean.' Jacca nudged her away. 'I can manage. Sit down and I'll bring your breakfast over.'

It took an hour before things were quiet enough for him to pour a mug of tea and join her.

'How's Connie?'

'Fast asleep.' Her shoulders drooped. 'I feel so guilty and confused.'

'Why?'

'Oh, gracious, where to start? Let's go with John. I'll be surprised if he ever speaks to me again. Then there's the fact I've been too wrapped up in my own little world to pay attention to my family. I've been shaken by all this,' Kaley explained. 'Life should about more than working, sleeping and eating.'

'If it helps I've gone through a lot of the same stuff since coming here and meeting you.' His admission made her smile. 'Does working through it together sound as good to you as it does to me?'

'It sure does.'

'I guess you're not busy if you've got time for that sort of thing?'

Jacca couldn't believe his eyes. Cash Harrison strolled into the café, smiling and unruffled in his well-tailored chinos and crisp white shirt.

'Where's Connie? She keeps avoiding me and it's urgent that I talk to her.'

'She's sleeping in her own bed. No thanks to you.' Kaley turned on him like a mother cat protecting her kittens.

'Me? I've no idea what you're talking about.'

'Why don't you take this into the kitchen?' Jacca suggested. 'I'll be out here if you need me. Keep the door open.'

'I assume you haven't spoken to Carlos Herrara today?' Kaley's first question clearly caught Cash out.

'Uh, I haven't been to the restaurant yet.'

Kaley zeroed in.

'Herrara is claiming you as his 'get out of jail' card.'

'Jail?' The colour drained from his face.

'He told the police you paid him a thousand dollars to abduct Connie and take her to that old house you own in East Nashville.' She gave a wry smile when he started to bluster.

'I'm taking a wild guess your plan was to swoop in to rescue her then persuade her to agree to your offer for the business?' Kaley pulled out her phone. 'Before I call the police I want to know why this development is so important to you.'

'Oh, now I'm done for.' Cash sunk down on one of the kitchen stools and clasped his head in his hands. 'I'm up to my neck in debt and my restaurant is on the ropes. Without the Dixieside scheme I'm finished.' He shrugged. 'If he stayed on board I might've survived.'

She hadn't noticed Jacca hovering in the doorway.

'Luiz heard a buzz that our friend here is too fond of the roulette table.'

A deep flush mottled Cash's face.

'But where are you getting the money from to gamble?' Kaley struggled to make sense of it all.

'He's probably employing the old robbing Peter to pay Paul trick and persuaded gullible investors to put money up front and promising to pay them back when the plan is a success,' Jacca explained. 'I would've been one of his stooges if I hadn't come to my senses. Is that right, Harrison? I expect his investors are turning the screws. Right?'

Cash stared at the floor and said nothing.

'Call the police, Kaley.'

It didn't take long to explain the situation to Alex Warner, the detective in charge of Connie's case.

'For what it's worth I genuinely cared for you.' Cash's steady gaze ignited a fleeting memory of the charming, confident man who once swept her off her feet. A rush of sadness swamped her to see him reduced to this quiet desperation.

'You had a lucky escape when you dumped me.'

'There was no luck involved. I was too smart to let you fool me for long.'

'You're right . . . but then you always were.' His voice broke and at that point, Detective Warner and a young policeman strolled in.

Moments later, Kaley and Jacca watched as Cash, pale-faced and haggard, was led outside, handcuffed to the young officer.

'We'll take him back to the station to be charged,' the detective explained. 'I'll need a statement from you both later.'

★ ★ ★

'Here we go.' Kaley set down a tray of tea and they sat down in the empty café. Along with the tea she had a plate of the lemon thyme shortbread he made early this morning.

'Right let's see if this is any good.' After breaking off a piece she studied the inside before taking a bite.

'I'd suggest chopping the thyme finer and doubling the amount of lemon rind. You might want to leave them in the oven for an extra two minutes next time because they're a little pale.'

'Cheeky madam. We'll make a baker out of you yet.' He watched her smile wobble. 'It's OK. It's not what you want. I get that. When I said I loved you there weren't any conditions.'

'I get that but . . . '

'But nothing.'

'So what's your plan?'

If he didn't step up now the moment could be lost. 'All I want is to make you happy.'

'That's simplistic.'

'I'm a simple man.' He shrugged. 'I think we could share a good life together and I'll do whatever it takes to make that happen.' Jacca registered Kaley's shock but ploughed on.

'If you want us to be involved in the Dixie Street renovation and the new restaurant that's what we'll do but if not I'll turn it over to someone else. You could do your freelance programming from wherever we end up.' He studied her, unable for once to work out what was going through her head.

'I'm cool with living here in the States and I can still work in Europe on a temporary basis if something interesting presents itself.'

'What about Sandy?'

'He'll be OK.' Jacca stared into her sparkling eyes. 'Tell me if I'm rushing things or if I've got the completely wrong idea about you . . . and us.' A flutter of panic zipped through him.

'Rushing? Maybe, but I've never been one to hang back and let life simply happen to me.' Kaley tilted him a brilliant smile. 'And I like 'us' very much.'

He hadn't realised he was holding his breath until he wasn't any longer.

'I really think I'd enjoy working on the renovation deal.' She looked slightly shamefaced.

'I needed to grow up to truly appreciate this town . . . and my family. This would be a perfect way to give something back.' Kaley burst into tears. 'Sorry.'

'No, I'm the one who should be sorry. You've been through enough the last twenty-four hours. I should've waited to say all those things.'

'Don't you dare apologise.' She jerked out of his arms and her voice was laced with the same feisty tone he remembered from the day they met.

'If you say sorry again I'll think you didn't mean it.'

'Of course I did! Don't tie me up in knots.' Jacca pulled her over to sit his lap. He wasn't foolish enough to believe they'd sorted everything out but ordered himself to trust that all would be well.

Kaley told herself the wave of insecurity engulfing her was nothing more than a natural slump after an emotional few days. She wouldn't see Jacca until later and judging by the smells wafting out of the kitchen her help wasn't needed in there.

'Oh, hi, is everything all right?' John wandered out, eating a scone.

'Yeah, of course why wouldn't it be?' She gulped down a sob. 'OK, that's a lie. Do you think Jacca and I are mad? I mean we love each other but long term?'

'Hey, it's OK. Life's not a neatly written programme with code to be tested and retested until it's perfect. I've discovered that being with Connie makes me a more rounded person.' His shy smile was tinged with pride. 'I'm pretty sure that works both ways.'

'Oh, John, you're a genius!' Kaley startled him by smacking a loud kiss on his cheek. 'I've been looking at all this the wrong way. Our differences are what makes 'us' work.'

'Hey, keep your hands off my man.' Connie's raucous laughter made them both jump. 'I heard all that nonsense. For heaven's sake just be honest with poor Jacca.'

'Stop being so smart both of you and go back to work.' She shooed them away. 'I need to think.'

★ ★ ★

The glittering topaz caught the sunlight streaming in through the window. Jacca stared at it hoping for inspiration.

Sandy lumbered back into the room, gasping for breath. He collapsed on the sofa in his sweat-soaked gym clothes and gulped down a bottle of water.

'Wow! When did you get that flashy thing?'

'You think it's too much?' Panic flooded through him again.

'Don't be an idiot. I didn't mean that literally.' Sandy grabbed the ring and examined it. 'Very nice. What's the plan for giving it to her?'

'I don't have one yet.' Jacca knew he sounded morose but he'd been awake half the night worrying over how and when to propose. In the darkest moments he had fretted over whether he should even propose at all. 'How are things with you and Helen?'

'We're very good friends.'

'And?'

'We've both been burned a few times and aren't keen to throw ourselves back in the fire.' Sandy rested his hands on his knees.

'Let's talk business for a minute. I've heard that Harrison's investors have all backed out and Nico thinks we'll be a shoo in with the planning commission.'

'That's good news but do you really want to do this? I'm talking about you personally, mate.' Jacca needed to be sure.

'Staying here in Franklin interests me, at least for a while. Apart from my family back in Cornwall I don't have any ties.'

'Do you want some?'

'Maybe.' Sandy looked thoughtful. 'The appeal is growing.'

'In that case I'm definitely in.'

'And Kaley?'

'She's still keen, too, but my decision stands even if she changes her mind.'

'Cool. I'll tell Nico.' Sandy whipped out his phone and fired off a text. Almost immediately it beeped with a reply.

'We're on for tonight at seven. His sous chef can take charge of dinner service.'

'Good deal. I think I'll follow your example and work off some energy in the gym.' He burst out laughing. 'That's a sentence I never expected to say in a million years.'

Sandy laughed and headed off for a shower, leaving Jacca alone with his thoughts.

* * *

'Are you ready?' Connie shook her blonde wavy hair out from its work ponytail. 'Mom's fixing dinner early so you can go to your mysterious meeting.'

Kaley ignored her sister's unsubtle attempt to find out where she was going. Least said the best until she had something definite to report.

'Mom wants to celebrate Dad's first treatment. According to the doctor he tolerated it well and if things continue he should see an improvement in his pain levels in a few weeks.'

'That's incredible. Come on let's go.' She would enjoy being with her family and leave the rest to fate.

Two Proposals

Several hours later she stared out of the taxi window and rested her hand against her stomach in an effort to quell her nerves. Kaley had forced down enough macaroni cheese and baked ham to forestall any pointed comments from her mother.

She intercepted more than one quelling glance from her father when Lorna's questions veered towards her future plans and whether they might involve Jacca.

At the restaurant she played for time and walked up instead of getting the lift. When she fixed on a smile and pushed the swing door open the three men gathered around a table at one end of the bar all glanced up.

'Hi, guys.' All of her nerves disappeared when her gaze locked with Jacca's. Something about the fact he was wearing the same baggy grey jumper, well-worn jeans and trademark red shoes as the day they met made things right.

'Come and join us.' Nico jumped up. 'Chardonnay?'

'Wonderful.' When she nabbed the chair next to Jacca it surprised her not to get a hug or a kiss. Something about the way he held himself, taut and unsmiling made her uneasy.

'Shall we get on?' Nico passed them each a piece of paper. 'This is the letter my attorney put together for the planning commission.' He skimmed through each point of the submission.

'So we're all agreed on pressing forward?'

Kaley's fingers brushed against Jacca's as the original document went around to be signed but there was no playful squeezing or fun today.

'Let's celebrate.' Nico opened a bottle of champagne and poured them each a glass. 'I whipped up some new tapas recipes earlier for y'all to try.' He rushed off towards the kitchen.

'I'm going to make a phone call,' Sandy announced. 'Be back in a minute.'

She waited for Jacca to say something. Anything.

'What's wrong?' Kaley's eyes drew him in. Today they were the colour of burnt butterscotch and shadowed with worry. 'Talk to me.'

If he dared to scoot his chair closer the thick, silky tumble of waves would be perfumed with her favourite hibiscus shampoo, laden with hints of the tropics and warm spices.

'I can't.' Jacca rushed to correct himself. 'Not here. Can we go somewhere to talk on our own when we're through? Please.'

'Sure.'

He kept a neutral expression on his face when he spied Sandy coming back and ignored it when his friend made the thumbs up and down sign behind Kaley's back.

'Here we go.' Nico set a large white platter loaded with colourful nibbles down on the table. 'I won't give you any details about what they all are because I want you to taste without any preconceived ideas.'

Kaley caught his eye and they both stifled a giggle as memories of their early, challenging times in the kitchen together flooded back.

It sent a surge of optimism soaring through him. Jacca was determined to whisk her out of there as soon as possible without being rude.

By nine o'clock they were back where it all began. He'd thought hard about where to suggest they go for their talk but the bakery was the obvious spot. Now he wasn't sure how to ease the conversation around to what he wanted to say.

'I was all out of sorts this morning. Questioning me. Questioning us.' Kaley beat him to it. 'Poor John got the brunt of it. After he listened to me rambling on the sweet guy pointed out something so obvious I wondered how I could have been that dumb.' A deep flush lit up her cheeks.

'Yeah, we're different and it's not goin' to be easy but that's life. We complement each other. Balance each other out.'

Jacca felt his grin spread from ear to ear. She'd put into words so many of the arguments that he'd planned to use if she didn't immediately say yes to his proposal.

'You won't get any argument from me.' Before his courage failed him he wriggled the small black velvet box out of his pocket and pushed his chair out of the way. Jacca dropped down on one knee.

'Kaleisha, I love you more than anything. Will you marry me?' He flipped the box open. 'If it makes any difference to your answer when you say yes you get this little bauble.' A local jeweller had helped him to design the large square cut yellow topaz surrounded by diamonds.

'Of course I will and I love you, too. Ring or no ring.' Her eyes shone as he slid it on her finger. 'Oh, it's beautiful. It's so unusual.'

'So are you.' Jacca cradled her face between his hands and indulged in a long, lingering kiss.

'My folks will be thrilled. Mom kept trying to bug me tonight about what my plans were and poor Daddy was shushing her.'

Jacca's cheeks burned, no matter how many icebergs he tried to think about.

'They knew?' Kaley's voice turned shrill. 'You sneaky thing.'

'Strictly speaking I didn't tell your mother but I rang your dad for a quick word and I'm sure she winkled it out of him. It was great to hear he's doing so much better already.'

'Yep, the doctor's incredibly hopeful. Nothing's one hundred percent sure, but of course we all know that.' Her radiant smile sizzled through him.

'You can say that again.' Jacca wrapped his arms around her. Sometimes talking wasn't necessary. Tomorrow, the day after and the one after that were time enough to tackle the other obstacles in their path.

★ ★ ★

The calendar insisted it was six months today since they got engaged but Kaley found that hard to believe.

'I just picked this up at City Hall.' Jacca was gleefully waving around a piece of paper. 'It's the official approval for the Dixie Street regeneration project.'

'Awesome. Now we can kick up a gear.'

'That's the plan.' His wide grin could barely be contained. 'I popped into 'Kurl up and Dye' yesterday and Jonathan told me his business is up about fifty percent and he's taken on another stylist.'

As soon as they submitted the proposal they formulated a marketing plan to get all of the established businesses working together to kick start interest in this neglected area of the city and it had been a huge success.

'A family who came in for breakfast yesterday said they wouldn't have known we were here if they hadn't spotted the new signs we put up along Main Street.'

An idea leapt into her head.

'We should round up Sandy and Nico to celebrate.'

'I'll give Nico a ring. Sandy already said he'd be over later.'

'Does he still insist he and Helen are simply 'good friends'?'

'Yes, and don't interfere.' He playfully wagged a finger at her.

'Me? I wouldn't dare.'

'Oh, yes? Like you didn't interfere with Connie and John?'

Kaley tossed her head.

'Come on, you've got admit that didn't do any lasting harm. I mean they have abandoned the bakery and run off on holiday for a week leaving us knee deep in scones again. If you're going to keep nagging me I'll move back to California and write gaming apps again.'

'You'd be miserable.'

Of course he was right. She'd happily left that life behind and was relishing the independent projects she worked on now.

'I might warn the Department of Homeland Security that you're an undesirable alien. You'll be packed off back to Cornwall on the next plane.'

'And who'll suffer the most if that

happens?' Jacca swept her up in his arms and strode back into the kitchen. He set her down on her feet as someone pounded on the front door.

'Who on earth is that now? We've still got half an hour before opening time.'

'I'll go and see.'

She followed him out when she heard Jacca shouting at someone.

'What are you doing here? Clear off, Harrison. You're breaking one of your bail conditions being here.'

'Yeah, I know.' Cash shoved a hand through his lank, unkempt hair. 'I wanted to apologise to Kaley and Connie. I'm trying to turn my life around and I'm desperate to try to put things right.'

'My sister's away.'

'We're about to make coffee — you'd better come on in.' Jacca's offer shocked her as much as Cash.

'Are you sure?'

'Yes.' He grasped Cash's arm and steered him inside. 'Sit down. Have you eaten?'

'Eaten?'

'Yes, you look like you're about to pass out.'

'I'll fix you something.' Kaley assumed Jacca had something in mind although couldn't imagine what it might be.

'It's safe. I've trained her. She won't poison you.'

'I bet she'd like to,' Cash mumbled.

She left the two men alone and struggled to concentrate on not messing up in the kitchen.

'Here you go. A cheddar and pear scone, prosciutto scrambled eggs and fresh fruit salad in a balsamic vinaigrette.' She set down the loaded plate. 'The coffee is almost ready.'

'Thanks.' Cash broke open the scone and popped in a large bite. 'Delicious. You've learned from a master. I couldn't make any better than that.'

'For once we agree on something.' Jacca made them all smile. 'Where are you living now?'

'Here and there.'

'I'm guessing you can't get a kitchen job?'

'What do you think?' Cash sounded resigned.

'Do you have a decent attorney?' Kaley asked.

'They've appointed a public defender because I'm bankrupt. I sold my house to pay some of my debts and my family has cut me off.' Cash shrugged. 'I can't blame them.'

Despite everything it didn't give her any pleasure to see him brought this low.

'Is there any chance of a plea deal? Perhaps instead of jail time they could get you into a treatment programme for your gambling problem and follow up with community service?'

'It's a possibility but . . . '

'What?'

'Connie would have to put in a good word for you?' Jacca's question hit home and Cash nodded.

'Yeah, but why should she? I'm not trying to make excuses but I never intended to hurt her or anyone else. The arson attempt was supposed to happen when no-one was there but he screwed up. I was in too deep to think straight about anything.'

'I'm willing to talk to her but I can't make any promises,' Kaley offered. 'Isn't there a programme you could get into while you're waiting for your case to go to court?'

'They're all too expensive.'

'We could pay.'

'No way! I couldn't possibly accept your help.'

'You can't afford to be proud right now.' Jacca shrugged. 'Take the offer before she changes her mind.'

'I will. Thank you.' Cash sighed and pushed away his empty plate. 'I'll get out from under your feet. You've got work to do.'

She couldn't let him disappear to walk the streets and probably sleep rough tonight.

'Connie is away for the rest of the week so why don't you crash in her flat while we check on getting you into a live-in treatment facility?'

Surprise and admiration flitted over

Jacca's face.

'Seriously?' Cash gasped. 'Why are you doing all this after the way I've behaved to you and your family?'

'Because she's soft hearted. Make the most of it.' Jacca's warning came with a faint smile. 'Kaley, why don't you take him upstairs to settle in while I get ready to open up the café?'

Happy the Bride

'You did what?' Connie shrieked. 'Are you out of your mind?' She leaned around and poked John's arm. 'Tell her she's lost her marbles.'

She should have taken Jacca's advice to break the news to her sister before they left the airport.

'It's only for tonight because Cash is moving into a rehab facility near Vanderbilt tomorrow. Mom and Dad say it'll be like old times to have us both at home.' Kaley caught a quiet glance pass between John and her sister.

'Fine. He can stay.'

While the going was good she explained their idea to try and keep Cash out of jail.

'Me? Speak up for him?' Connie rolled her eyes. 'I suppose I can but don't ask for anything else. Has Mom killed the fatted calf for our return?'

'I believe it's a fatted roast chicken. Jacca's meeting us there.'

'Mom tells me you're making wedding plans.' Her sister's eyes sparkled. 'If you stick me in some ugly puffball of a dress I'll never forgive you.'

Kaley was afraid to admit they wanted the quietest wedding in history.

Jacca still had hang-ups about the fact that his mother drove her parents deep into debt to finance her dream wedding but the marriage disintegrated before their first anniversary.

Should she tell her sister the story behind their decision? She lost her nerve.

As soon as Kaley managed to pin down Jacca on his own, she looked him straight in the eye.

'I've got two main questions,' she said slowly. 'The first is whether we're going to visit Cornwall and meet your mother before or after the wedding?'

Put on the spot he wasn't sure how to respond but she didn't rush him.

'I think after will be best.' Jacca guessed he'd answered the right way when Kaley gave a tight smile and a nod.

The strained relationship with his

mother would make the introductions hard enough without throwing the stress of a wedding into the mix.

'Number two isn't exactly a question because as far as the scale of the wedding is concerned I suggest we find a compromise between my mother's desire to replicate Harry and Meghan's royal shindig and your inherent preference for a blink-and-you-miss-it variety.'

'Perfect. As long as you're happy.' Jacca nuzzled a trail of kisses down her neck but she playfully pushed him away.

'This isn't getting a plan together.'

He prepared to pull a rabbit out of his hat.

'What about holding it at Nico's restaurant? I happen to know they're licensed to hold weddings.'

'That would be awesome. You're a genius.' Kaley's smile dazzled him.

'Are you sure it'll be . . . enough for you?'

'You're enough for me. The rest is icing on the cake.' Her eyes gleamed. 'Or should that be butterscotch glazed coffee bars? You know we've got to serve them?'

'Whatever you want, sweetheart.' Jacca kissed her. 'I've got everything I need right here.'

★ ★ ★

'There's still time to change your mind.' Sandy strolled in brandishing a bottle of Jack Daniels and two glasses. 'I thought we needed a drop of courage.'

'All you've got to do is produce two rings at the correct time and amaze everyone with a witty heartfelt speech,' Jacca teased his old friend.

'No problem.' He set the drinks on the table and retrieved a white envelope from his pocket. 'This came for you this morning. It's postmarked Cornwall.'

'Hand it over then.' A lump formed in his throat as he stared at the familiar writing. Jacca ripped open the envelope and pulled out a card that was decorated with silver bells and horseshoes.

'It's from my mum. She read about

our wedding in the newspaper and wanted to wish us well.' How stupid was he? It should've been obvious that with his high profile there was a good chance their big day would be reported in the media. 'She hopes we'll come to visit her when we have time.'

'That's good, isn't it?'

'I suppose.'

'She's all the family you've got, Jax. It'll make Kaley happy.' Sandy poured the drinks. 'Cheers, mate. You getting married certainly wasn't part of the plan when we rolled into town back in January.'

They clinked glasses.

* * *

'I didn't expect to say this but you were right.' Lorna's eyes shimmered with emotion. 'It's beautiful.'

As soon as Kaley tried it on she knew it was 'the one'. The short, white lace dress with its soft, flirty ruffle around the hemline was a perfect contrast to her rich, dark skin and the scattering of dia-manté sprinkles caught the light every time she moved.

'I love your hair.' Her mother touched the upswept mass of waves pinned with tiny diamond clips. 'Jacca will be a goner when he sees you.'

'That's the plan.' Kaley smiled. 'Where's Connie? She'd better not be late.'

'Are you talking about me again? Oh wow!' Her sister stopped in the door. 'That poor man is toast. Do I meet with your approval?' Connie did a twirl. Slim cut ice-blue silk. Strapless. Equally short. Nothing about the dress screamed bridesmaid.

'I love it.' Kaley threw her arms around her sister. 'And you.' She glanced over her shoulder. 'Come here, Mama.' The three of them linked arms and for a few precious seconds they soaked up the love between them. 'How's Daddy hold-ing up?'

'He's doin' good. I forced him to take a nap this afternoon.' Lorna kissed

Kaley's cheek. 'He'll bawl when he sees you. Come on, let's find him.'

Five minutes later the only thing that stopped her from falling apart when Spencer reacted exactly as her mother predicted was a mental picture of black mascara tracks inching down her face and ruining her make-up.

★ ★ ★

Jacca almost fell to his knees when Kaley appeared on her father's arm. Beautiful didn't come close to describing how she looked tonight.

Within a few short minutes he heard the best words ever.

'By the power vested in me by the state of Tennessee I now pronounce you man and wife. You may kiss your bride.'

At last.

Jacca linked his arm through hers and they walked together back down the makeshift aisle. One end of the restaurant had been turned into the ceremony space and the wall of windows left uncovered

to show off the full beauty of the sparkling night sky.

Kaley's eyes glowed and she lifted his
hand in the air.

'Let's get this party started!'

He had heard the ridiculous notion
that most couples were too nervous and
excited to eat at their wedding reception
but it wasn't a problem for them. Nico's
food was too delicious to miss out on.

'Go on, you want to check it out, don't
you?' Kaley caught him out giving the
dessert table a longing glance.

Jacca snatched a quick kiss and hurried over to see Helen. She had created
a wonderful display ranging from tropical fruit tarts topped with edible flowers
to divine miniature Jamaican mango
cheesecakes decorated with gold leaf.

Kaley had taken it for granted they
would serve butterscotch bars but he'd
collaborated with Helen to surprise her
by turning the recipe into an incredible
five-tier work of art to rival any wedding
cake. Out of the blue he caught Kaley's
eye across the room.

'Go back to your bride. You don't want to be in trouble before the ink is dry on the marriage certificate.' Helen shooed him off.

'Sorry, I didn't mean to stay that long.' His apology made Kaley smile.

'Don't worry I know where I rank in importance. Second to a cake.'

'Helen said it's time for us to cut it.'

They joined Nico and Helen and after they made a ceremonial cut he pulled off a shard of golden butterscotch and held it out for her to bite.

'Oh, heavens, now I remember why I married you.' Her twinkling eyes matched the sparkling diamonds in her hair. 'Ready to dance?' Jacca swung her into his arms.

'Let's do this.'

Plenty to Celebrate

'Wow. I knew it would be lovely from the pictures you showed me but . . . '

Words failed Kaley as she stared across the rugged cliffs at Land's End and out to the sparkling blue ocean.

He had kept their honeymoon destination a secret until they reached the Nashville airport the morning after their wedding and produced airplane tickets to London.

Once they arrived he was even more tentative in suggesting they spent most of their time in Cornwall. Jacca warned her the weather might be damp and rainy but so far they had enjoyed four picture-perfect warm sunny days.

'Should we get going? You said it'll take an hour and we're supposed to be in Truro by three o'clock.'

Last night she persuaded him to call his mother but he said very little afterwards except to warn her not to expect too much.

They said very little on the drive and she sensed him retreat inside himself.

'Has your mom lived here very long?' Kaley peered out at the whitewashed bungalow with its neat, well-tended garden.

'I bought it for her about five years ago. I grew up in a small village about ten miles away but when I offered to help her move she preferred to be closer to the town.'

A thin grey-haired woman appeared on the front doorstep and raised her hand in a tentative wave.

'Shall we get out?' So far he hadn't made any effort to move.

'I suppose so.'

When they stood at the garden gate Kaley begged him to smile.

'Welcome to Cornwall, my 'andsome. My boy was right when he said you're a pretty one.'

'Thank you, Mrs Hawken. It sure is great to meet you.'

'Call me Ethel, please, you're family now.' Her smile wobbled. 'I've got the kettle boiling but I don't suppose you're a tea drinker. I've got instant coffee or cold orange squash if prefer it.'

'I'd love a cold drink although squash is a new one on me. It sounds like another language clash to add to my list.'

'The garden's looking nice.' Jacca's compliment appeared to startle his mother. 'Are you still doing all the work yourself?'

'I take care of the flowers and Mr Edgerton next door mows the grass.' A faint blush tinged her sallow skin. 'I make him a pasty every Saturday in return.'

'That's an awesome deal.' Kaley smiled. 'I've totally fallen in love with your Cornish pasties.'

'Come on in and sit down while I see to the tea.' Ethel refused any help. 'Take your pretty bride in the front room.'

Jacca was unnaturally quiet but she didn't try to tease him out of it as they sat together on the stiff, blue velour sofa.

'Help yourself to a scone, love.' Ethel set a plate down on the coffee table. 'I'm afraid they're not home-made.' She gave

Jacca an apologetic nod. 'My efforts wouldn't be good enough for someone.'

'That's daft, Mum. I've never said that.' Kaley glared at him. 'I'm sorry, I never realised you felt that way.'

'I've no idea where my boy got his talent from.' Ethel mused.

'I contacted my father the other day.' Kaley stared at Jacca in shock, unable to believe what he just blurted out. His father was the one subject he swore he wouldn't talk about today. 'He didn't want to know, Mum.'

'Rob's a fool.' His mother shook her head. 'I'm sorry.'

'You've nothing to be sorry for, but I do . . .' His courage faltered until Kaley squeezed his hand and her comforting touch gave him the strength to keep going. 'I blamed you for everything and that wasn't fair.'

'We all make mistakes.' Kaley explained some of her own family challenges. 'Maybe you can both find a way to draw a line under the past and move on?'

'I'd love nothing better.' His mother's eyes filled with tears.

'Me too,' Jacca admitted. 'I'm really sorry we can't stay and talk more today but we've got a long drive up to Reading. We're staying there tonight before we fly back to Nashville tomorrow afternoon. Would it be all right if we came back again soon?'

'That would be lovely. I've got a nice little spare bedroom so you could stay here if you wanted.'

'We'd really like that.' Jacca cleared his throat. 'Maybe one day you could come to see us in Nashville?'

'Oh, I don't know — it's an awful long way and I've never been on a plane.' Ethel's face heated. 'It's not that I don't want to.'

'We understand. It's a long journey and travelling sure isn't much fun these days.' Kaley sympathised.

'I'm some glad you came and brought your lovely wife.'

'Me too.' Jacca was amazed to genuinely mean that. For the first time it was hard to say goodbye and they didn't say much until they were in the car and back on the main road.

'You're amazing.' He smiled across at Kaley. 'I couldn't have done that without you.'

'I'm just happy things turned out better than we expected.'

'You mean than I expected. Don't you dare say any more now or I might turn soft and unmanly. That could be downright dangerous while I'm driving.'

'Mouth sealed shut.' All he could think was that being married to this incredible woman was the best thing ever.

* * *

Jacca gazed at the cloudless blue sky. Thankfully the weather forecaster's prediction of heavy rain hadn't materialised.

'Come on, I need some smiles from you guys.' The photographer ordered them around and Jacca took up his assigned spot between Kaley and Nico. They stuck their brand new shovels in

238

the dirt and grinned for the camera.

The empty lot at the end of Dixie Street had been cleared before winter set in and now it was March and time to break ground on their new enterprise. Nico's small upscale restaurant would include a training programme for young chefs who couldn't afford culinary school and instead of a hotel the regeneration plans included twenty affordable housing units and a community centre.

Jacca checked out the assembled crowd, an interesting mix of the media, local politicians, business people and the simply curious.

'It's great to see y'all here.' Kaley took charge of the microphone. 'Franklin has a great future and our new development intends to be part of its carefully measured growth.

'Now I think we'll leave the heavy digging work to the professionals and you can join us at my family's bakery for some warming hot chocolate and our famous Butterscotch Bars.'

He had given in to Sandy's constant

nagging and started a small business to make the butterscotch bars more widely available. When they promoted them at the Nashville food festival, local celebrity chef Simone Guerlain had fallen in love with them and now the bars were selling as fast as they could make them.

Jacca pulled Kaley into his arms for a kiss.

'I love you. I'd say we've done a good six months' work.' He rested his hand on her flat stomach, protecting the secret they'd sworn to keep to themselves until Easter. His mother surprised them at Christmas by announcing that she'd applied for her first passport and intended to visit in the spring.

'For goodness' sake keep your hands off each other. You're married now,' Sandy teased them. 'Of course you won't have time for all that when the baby arrives.'

'Shush.' Jacca was relieved to see no-one else was close enough to overhear. 'How did you guess?'

'I'm one of seven kids, remember. I've seen my mum pregnant enough times to know the signs. Don't worry, my lips will stay sealed if you bribe me with a handful of butterscotch bars.'

'Won't the dragon lady kick you out if she smells sugar on your breath?'

'Very funny.'

He hadn't been convinced Sandy would stick to his lifestyle changes back in London but his old friend looked great.

'Is Helen here?'

'No, she's working. I'll see her later.'

'How are things with you two?'

'We're good as we are.'

Jacca shut up when Kaley threw him a warning glare.

'Hey you lot, we're supposed to be glad-handing our supporters.' Nico hurried over to join them. 'If you don't drag your lovely wife down to the bakery I will.'

'Don't even think about it.' He seized Kaley's hand. 'Let's go. I want to shout to the whole world that you're having my baby,' he whispered. They had agreed to wait until Ethel arrived but he was like a child on Christmas Eve.

'Don't you dare!'

They strolled along Dixie Street and slowed down outside number 24. A couple of months ago they bought the modest red brick house and hoped to finish refurbishing it before their baby arrived in early September.

'We're snowed under.' Lorna was standing outside the bakery yelling at them. 'You didn't warn us half of Williamson County would turn up. I told your daddy not to overdo it but he's ignoring me.'

'I'm happy he's well enough to help. You've got Connie and John serving, too, right?'

'Yeah but he's not much use, bless him.'

'What about Cash?' Her mother pursed her lips. 'Isn't he doing a good job?'

'He's working harder than anyone but you know what they say about leopards not changing their spots.'

Kaley couldn't be too hard on her

mother because she was dubious when Jacca suggested employing him, so far she was happy to be proved wrong.

'Let's eat cake and celebrate.' She hooked one arm through her mother's elbow and Jacca took hold of her other arm.

Celebrating life was a great place to start.

We do hope that you have enjoyed reading this large print book.

Did you know that all of our titles are available for purchase?

We publish a wide range of high quality large print books including:
Romances, Mysteries, Classics
General Fiction
Non Fiction and Westerns

Special interest titles available in large print are:
The Little Oxford Dictionary
Music Book, Song Book
Hymn Book, Service Book

Also available from us courtesy of Oxford University Press:
Young Readers' Dictionary
(large print edition)
Young Readers' Thesaurus
(large print edition)

For further information or a free brochure, please contact us at:
Ulverscroft Large Print Books Ltd.,
The Green, Bradgate Road, Anstey,
Leicester, LE7 7FU, England.
Tel: (00 44) 0116 236 4325
Fax: (00 44) 0116 234 0205

Penny can't wait to go on the holiday of a lifetime with her best friend, Angela. But then comes some terrible news: her father has had a heart-attack. Now she will have to spend the summer looking after her parents' little seaside shop instead. That wouldn't be so bad but the neighbouring LoPrice supermarket has its eyes on the property. And Penny isn't sure what to make of the assistant manager, Graham Fraser. He's young, good-looking — and very ambitious.

BEYOND HER DREAMS

Gail Richards

England, 1848. Housemaid Alice is taken from the big house she works in to be the only servant to Mrs Younger. The first person she meets is Daniel, whose friendly face she remembers in the dark, lonely days that follow. She dreams of romance but Daniel has a sweetheart — hasn't he? Then Mrs Younger disappears and it's up to Alice to find her. Will Daniel help or is he too interested in someone else?

A SUITABLE COMPANION

Philippa Carey

Earl Barton's daughter's new governess is collected from the stagecoach stop. However, the next morning they discover Clara Thompson is the wrong young lady — she had been expecting to be companion to a Lady Sutton. But Lady Sutton refuses to exchange her for the intended governess! They have to keep Clara on to help them with the tantrum-prone young Lady Mary while they find a replacement governess. However, could it be that the wrong young lady turns out to be the earl's right young lady?

THE SUMMERHOUSE GHOST

Camilla Kelly

Lizzie is thrilled when her theatre company gets the chance to put on an open-air production at a Georgian country house. As soon as she sees the property she's enchanted by it — and by two of the residents: Griffin, and his foster son, Oscar.

But the house has secrets, and something within it starts to threaten the play, Lizzie's new relationships, and her safety. Something in the house wishes her harm . . .

THE DUCHESS OF SYDNEY

Dawn Knox

Convicted of a crime she did not commit, and sentenced to the colonies in Australia, Georgiana had lost all hope . . . until she met Francis Brooks, Lieutenant on the transport ship and tasked with protecting her. Would she ever unravel all the secrets that kept them apart, and would she ever be free again — free to be herself, and free to love?